I0772285

LIVIN' LA VIDA LOBA

A Selena Sol-Valencia
Episodio 1

LIVIN' LA VIDA LOBA
A Selena Sol-Valencia Episodio 1
by
ANGELICA MARTINEZ

Livin' La Vida Loba A Selena Sol-Valencia Episodio One is a work of fiction. Names, characters, places, and incidents are the product of the author's imagination or are used fictitiously. Any resemblance to actual persons, living or dead, events, or locales is coincidental.

Published in the United States by
Four Elements Press LLC, New Jersey.

To request permission, contact
contact@fourelementspress.com

Cover design and interior design by My Lan Khuc (LaolanArt)
Edited by Alexander Anthony Casillas

ISBN 978-1-965996-31-7 (Hardcover)
ISBN 978-2-965996-30-0 (Paperback)
ISBN 978-1-965996-32-4 (Ebook)

Edition One
Published by Four Elements Press
FourElementsPress.com

LIVIN' LA VIDA LOBA

by

Angelica Martinez

FOUR
ELEMENTS
PRESS

Contents

1

NEWSFLASH: WE DON'T ALL LOOK ALIKE!

Contrary to stereotypes, there's no one way to be Mexican. Some of us pass for white, black, Asian, or Indigenous, but most of us look like a mix of some variation. My family, dancing in a cramped mess of kaleidoscopic greens, purples, and golds, are proof of that, as they dig their heels into the in-house dance floor separating me and where I hope Mom is lurking. I hunt for her tight, silver ballerina-bun like it's a swan in a sea of parrots, elbowing my way through fire-engine red feathers and hair colors, growing more annoyed every second with my 'oh-so glorious' quinceañera. But nothing could be worse than becoming a woman with *no* power, and according to Tía Marisol's inability to whisper, that's exactly what I am. Proven by the fact I'm now... *moving!?*

Mom's across the dancefloor, basking in the success of her party planning production and smiling her iconic 'everything's great in the universe' smile. Even though everything in *my* universe is being stolen from me. My whole past and my whole future, gone. Why spend my entire childhood in Santa Ana, just to move me *before I even finish high school?*

I can't put Mom up against Martha Stewart in my head tonight. I can't give her the championship she deserves for her hard work. Not even the smile lines of her cheeks as she talks or the bright red lipstick she picked out for tonight are enough to cool the boiling inside me. Every clink, clank, and shuffle feels right on top of my eardrum, and every molecule from inside and outside the house overpowers my olfactory, causing my already hyperactive brain to dance twelve dances at once. But I can't even take a step without another body getting in my way.

Leaving the snack table, Mom moves her average height and above average weight gracefully out of sight. I've always been her revelling shadow, behind her as she lights up every room she enters, leaving me unaccustomed to so much attention.

"Selena, happy birthday! Oh my, you look just like Graciela! You're growing up so fast," says Ron, an older Hawaiian coworker of my mom. Of course getting in my way.

"Thank you," I say, sliding past him as best I can.

He's always around, and everyone's always really happy to see him. But every time I see him, I wonder why he's there. Social family-outings make *me* want to stay in my *room.*

Especially when the alternative is being strapped into a dress that makes me look like a purple French-patisserie confection. And nothing against Ron, but I hate when people say I look like my mom. Sure, we have the same mouth and both wear black framed glasses, but my skin is way more tan. I have long, thick, curly black hair that frizzes in rebellion against the slightest humidity, just as much as it does when the Santa Ana winds come and save us from the aggressive summer heat. But, when you're a girl, I guess it's more flattering for people to say you look like your mom over your dad, who I can picture only because of the old photo pressed into my journal.

"Happy quinceañera, my little adult, princesa," my tía Marisol says to me, but I elbow past her without a word. Maybe the nudge was more aggressive than I intended, but I have to get to Mom before I blow up on anyone else and ruin everything.

I always felt really bad for the girls historically traded through marriage for goats or cows against lavish backdrops of parties and flowers and gifts. Back then, quinces were the precursor to actual weddings. All to rub the world in a girl's face before she had the chance to be herself and find her own path. At least now, girls get to keep their envelopes full of cold, hard cash, even if the world is still just as threatening.

But the cultural rite of passage my mom hoped would ground me to my Mexican roots and keep me far away from turning into, what she called, a *coconut* (brown on the outside, white on the inside), might be telling me I'm not made for life as the typical Mexican woman. She already tells me I read too many books written by 'dead, white British ladies,' and she's not wrong! Every chance I get, I sink back into the classics by Jane Austen, Mary Shelley, and the Brontë sisters.

If not for my friend Sophia, books would truly be my only friends. Well, now Sophia's a friend I *used* to have. And on top of it all, that swaggering, skinny-hipped, papi chulo Gabriel, my long-time crush, is moving, too. To Texas. And if Tía Marisol is right, Mom's moving us to the middle of nowhere, Vacaville. Population: my tío, who I barely know.

The party seethes with squeaky shoes, the burn of perfume, and the hint of body odor as I squeeze through tables and chairs. Sardines shoehorned into tiny tins have more space than us. Tías are gossiping about tíos being drunk and sobbing to the heart pulling ballads of Vicente Fernández. When I finally reach Mom at the drink table, she's pouring herself a glass of punch for the first time all day and laughing at something my tía Leticia said, but I can't wait for her to finish pouring. I grab her by the wrist and pull, dragging her into the kitchen in a hurry.

"We're moving!?" I shriek, once we're both through the swinging door.

"Calm down, mi vida," Mom implores, fixing her bun in the magnetic mirror stuck to the refrigerator. "Come here," she says, grabbing at the air in my direction for me to get closer.

"Ah, salio la sopa," Tía Marisol says, poking her head around the kitchen door, with a, 'tsk, tsk, tsk,' that sends me to the edge.

"Marisol, dejanos un momentito," Mom says, and we're alone again as the swinging door shudders closed.

"Why didn't you tell me?" I ask, fumbling over thoughts and words against the buzz of my rising anxiety. "I had to hear through family gossip? Shouldn't I be the first to know?" I shake.

"Tío Julio needs help with the finances. He only has two months before he loses the family farm," Mom says, trying to comfort me with her eyes over the frames of her glasses.

It always feels like she knows exactly what she wants to say, even when she looks like she's still trying to understand what's going through my head.

"And you thought I wouldn't have an opinion about moving? Or what? My opinion doesn't matter? Mom, I'm fifteen! I deserve some say about this. God, I can't think with these stupid bobby pins!"

I dig for the pins jammed into my scalp, restoring the blood flow to my brain with every pin I slip out.

"Mija, lower your voice. Our guests might hear," Mom says, shushing me in panic.

"No," I growl.

Mom steps back, and looks... afraid of me? Mom, who never fears anything because of our 'Indigenous blood,' afraid?

"What... ?" I ask, feeling fear come over me, too.

"You need space, Selena," Mom says, lowering her gaze and turning away.

I'd never seen her back away like it. For a second generation Mexican American, una Chicana, who proudly graduated from a PhD nursing program into a career, backing down isn't in her vocabulary.

"A fifteen year old woman, with the strength of our family, needs her space, Selena. You'll understand, soon."

Then Sophia hurtles through the kitchen door, looking unsure about what she walked into, but with me in her sights.

"Let's take a minute away from the party," Sophia says, and I let her move me as she guides my shoulder. But I'm not calm, not satisfied, and still boiling with an anger that won't tamp down.

In my Pepto-bismol pink room, I open a window and let in the taco-truck scented breeze as Sophia plops herself on my bed, watching me with her chayote green eyes. The smell of tacos, arroz con pollo, and tortillas, soothes me. A puff of ajo, chile, oregano, and cilantro drifts in, too. My mom knows how to cater a mean party. I almost feel guilty for not enjoying myself, but *moving!* I might be in shock, but I wouldn't know the difference.

"Is everything alright? You're usually so soft spoken with your mom," Sophia says, as she tucks a loose curled tendril of hair behind her ear.

Sophia's hair is always corralled securely with rhinestone-studded pins, accentuating her perfectly oval face. She's pretty and bold, in the quiet way that I usually am. I can't replace Sophia with... my tío Julio. It hurts so bad that I don't even want to talk about it with her.

"You don't understand what it's like," I say, scratching more pins off my scalp and looking at her through my vanity mirror. "Your mom accepts your bipolar, lets you change your hair color, and isn't as strict. I'm done trying to be my mom's compliant *perfect daughter!* What does trying get me?!"

"What did she do that's so bad?" Sophia asks, chewing on her lower lip and staring at me in the mirror.

The traditional cobalt blue Mexican dress she's wearing cinches the taut physique of her upper body, contrasting the embroidered rose pattern against her bright, fair skin. The smell of lavender off her body fills the room as if coming from the rainbow of flowers across her chest. The smell of her alone is usually enough to calm me. She says it's one of the perks of doing a family's worth of laundry every week.

Sophia honors the duties of 'the only daughter' in a way I never could, and she's not even Mexican.

"Does it even matter?" I say. "She thinks she's justified in making huge decisions without me. Decisions that impact everyone and everything. Even you."

"What do you mean?" she asks, even more curious now. "What's so bad?"

"She's selling our house and moving us eight hours away! To the middle of freaking nowhere!" I flounce down on my bed with a huff.

"What?! You're moving? That's not fair! Why?" Sophia reaches to comfort me, and I practically jump out of my skin at her touch.

"Don't touch me!" I cry. The graze of her fingers feels like a cat clawing into my skin, and somehow the room starts spinning. I can't focus on the pain in Sophia's eyes. I can barely breathe, as my dress tightens like a barbarian torture device against the backdrop of blasting DJ speaker Bachata.

"Okay well, when you're ready to join your party, you know where to find me," Sophia pouts, turning away from me and getting up to leave.

"I just... I need air," I say after her, sweating bullets through my dress and feeling wet as I get up to leave, too.

Outside my room, is... everyone. Mom and Sophia, in front. Sophia, holding a giant ice cream cake she must've taken from Mom. Mint chocolate chip and chocolate cake! The exact one I asked for two months ago, and the one I'd forgotten about in the craziness of getting the house and myself ready for the party.

"Feliz cumpleaños a ti, mi vida," Mom says, and the pleading look in her eye for me to smile back hurts my heart.

But, I'm not in control anymore.

"Estas son las mañanitas / Que cantaba Rey David!"

Everyone's singing *Las Mañanitas*, the Mexican birthday song, but my heart beat is racing at a new thump that fills my ears.

"Hoy, por ser día de tu santo / Te las cantamos aquí," they sing.

My flesh burns like a blowtorch, and my brain freezes over.

"Despierta, mi bien / Despierta, mira que ya amaneció," they sing.

My chest puffs, shallow and crushed by the invisible weight of an elephant.

"Ya los pajaritos cantan / La luna ya se metió," they sing.

I gasp for breath.

"Qué linda está la mañana / En que vengo a saludarte," they sing.

Their bodies, everywhere. Pumping with thick, Mexican, Indigenous blood.

"Venimos todos con gusto / Y placer a felicitarte," they finish.

And in the heat of everything, I transform fully into something else. Hair covers my arms, hands, and CHIN? My muscles burst through the dress, stretching it to tattered threads around coarse bushels of hair.

Everyone gasps and murmurs and shouts at each other about what to do, as the DJ slides into "Loba," by Shakira. But nobody really knows what to do when a daughter, niece, and cousin turns into a werewolf.

Mom presses her fingers on my wrist, checking my pulse. But everywhere she touches burns with the sting of newly formed muscle tissue. Even the follicles of my new, tough, and wiry hair burn with a sensitivity that makes me want to growl.

"Get away!" I shout, swatting everyone back before swallowing a... howl? Sophia stands behind my mom, in jaw-dropped shock.

"Mija, I'm going to need you to calm down!" Mom says, raising her voice.

"No!" I growl, and the numbness of my brain turns to pain. I clamber forward, reaching for the ice cream cake in Sophia's hands to cool my burning head. Chairs fly as I struggle for control of my tender limbs, and screams ring around the room as I slam my fists down on the ice cream cake. Sophia scrambles back.

Everyone's rushing for the back door, and I, too, remember the coolness of the night from the breeze through the window. If I could just get outside to cool down, maybe I'd feel better. Then I notice the unicorn ice sculpture by the door, gleaming with drops of ice cold water, and I start making my way across the tables, chairs, and people between me and it.

"Everyone, get away from the ice unicorn, NOW!" Mom warns, somehow always knowing what I'm thinking.

Family and friends scurry back the other way if they haven't already made it outside, and I hurl myself at the unicorn sculpture. I soar through the air. The unicorn crashes into a thousand pieces, and I'm left in a fury of pain and rage atop the collapsed table. I howl again, desperate for some relief. I scramble against the slick floor, somehow using all four of my limbs as feet, and make it out the back door and into the cold night.

Outside, the moon is full and bright in the sky over the house. I howl and howl, until my howls wane in and out between the wail of sirens. Before I forfeit to the fatigue of my crying.

2

FIFTY-ONE FIFTY'D

I wake with a jerk to sirens spiralling overhead. The back of the ambulance is bright white. Mom's on one side, with an EMT on the other, but the proverbial bus I feel hit by is nowhere to be seen. The EMT pulls at my arm and straps a blood pressure cuff around my bicep. It gets tight, the way my dress... used to strangle me at the waist. Now, it feels baggier than a hospital gown.

The cuff inflates, and the pump hisses with the air pumping back through the cord. Nobody knows what to say. They're both floating their gaze around the cab to avoid eye contact with me.

"We were having a good time," Mom says. "I don't know what happened. It's her fifteenth birthday. I thought young adults were supposed to be easier. Then, suddenly she goes ballistic and starts destroying everything."

My cheeks burn, "You're lying, she's lying! She's a liar!" I scream.

"Excuse me, I wasn't addressing you," the EMT says.

"You're a liar!" I say. I don't know why. My mom's telling the truth. The EMT's just doing his job. I'm just... holding on?

Fatigue washes over me again, and I lay back baffled, the adrenaline coming over me like a driver on the Autobahn. Going as fast as I can and fearing, at every second, a crash. Then, blackness.

When I open my eyes again, I'm still strapped to the stretcher. Now, on my way through the hospital. Someone's checking my vitals again. The inane beeping of the machines fills my head, putting me in a spiral of vintage video game memories. Like Ms. Pac-Man, but less fun. The screen reads 150 over 90 for my blood pressure, as I fade in and out.

"Is her blood pressure normally this high? She should be less than one-twenty over eighty!" the nurse with the Eugene Levy eyebrows barks at my mom.

"Don't talk to my mom like that! She's a nurse, too!" I snap, shooting him a steely gaze.

"Is she normally this rude?" the stylish platinum blonde asks from the other side of the sterile hospital room.

"Not this openly, and not to strangers," answers my befuddled mom, and she's right. I don't know what's going on with me.

They wheel me into *Observation*, or 'fifty-one fifty,' they call it. They strip me out of the threads of my dress and take my phone, along with my necklace, earrings, and the rest of the hair pins tangled in the nest of my hair.

Mom's in a corner of the room. A solitary tear rolls down her cheek. Typically, this would break me. As much as I like to put on a front that nothing phases me, I love my mom desperately. Yet, somehow I feel no connection to her. I feel like a genuine stranger in my body. Like I'm in the middle of an out-of-body experience. A gaping nothingness fills my chest. No pain. No rage. Just emptiness.

"We'll keep your daughter here for seventy-two hours so we can evaluate her. We'll notify you if she continues to be a danger to herself and others, and if we have to move her again," the platinum blonde says, as she writes something on a clipboard.

"Do you know when I can see her again?" Mom says, as she wipes the unfallen tears from her eyes.

"We have to do the evaluation first. You're welcome to go home and get some rest," says the nurse kindly. "We'll call you."

Sucking up all of her Mexican-Indigenous strength, Mom squeezes my hand, and says something I don't recognize. Then leaves.

I'm alone. Left to my own thoughts. It's what I needed all night. But… it's not a room alone. Curtains separate the hospital beds, and I can see slender legs in grippy yellow socks poking out on the bed next to mine.

"Hey, what's your name?" I ask, trying to be polite.

"No talking!" growls a nurse, hidden somewhere on the other side of the curtain. "To assess the individual's mental state and stabilize them, staff and patients are not to engage in conversation as it may worsen their condition or hinder the evaluation."

I give up, and try to lean into the bed to get comfortable, but the beads of sweat rolling down my forehead puddle on the scratchy scrubs, making the fabric the itchiest thing I've ever worn. I ask to use the toilet and decide to take advantage of the shower stall while I'm at it. I strip down and sigh as the cold water sizzles against my skin, washing away everything I want to forget about the day.

After the shower, I check myself out in the mirror. No longer a girl, but a woman. I don't recognize either, in the steam polished reflection. Mascara streaks her cheeks and eyes like charcoal buttons as I stare back at the emptiness of my body. Naked and shivering, I cover my chest and crack open the door.

"May I get some towels?" I ask.

"Sure thing," the nurse sighs, and grabs a couple of towels from the stack behind her.

I pat myself dry in the bathroom, hearing voices through the door as I take my time.

"We always get weird ones on the Full Moon," a passing nurse says.

Was I actually howling at the moon? Or crying?

The fresh hospital gown is refreshing after the original scratchy scrubs. Back in bed, hunger claws at my insides. Even though I ate at the party, my stomach feels ravenous.

"Can I get a snack, please?" I ask the next nurse I see.

"I'll see what I can do," she says back.

"Did you see she got a pedicure for the psych ward? That was certainly a choice," says a nasty voice from somewhere.

"Forget the pedicure. Did you see her hair when she first got here? She was in a whole getup, too," says a judgy second voice.

"Get out of my head!" I say, shocking myself, but nobody else in the room flinches. I quietly bring the blanket to my chin and clamp the pillow over my ears, but still the voices come.

Three nights later, I still haven't slept a full night despite the cocktail of meds they give me. It takes the edge off for sure, but I'm still on high alert. Like I'm in danger.

One night, I see a black dog stalking the nurses down the hall. The dog stops and stares back at me, but it escapes the nurses' glance.

"Why is there a big black dog here?" I ask a night nurse one night.

"Only service dogs are allowed in the hospital, and none fit that description, as far as I know," she says.

No matter how many pills I take, I see the dog around every corner. It's never aggressive or menacing, but curious. The night it turned and looked me in the eyes I felt seen and almost recognized. I felt like it knew me, even if I was learning just how much I didn't know myself.

"Nurse Charlotte, is it normal to see things after not sleeping for a few days?"

"It's fairly common to hallucinate while experiencing insomnia," she replies, with little concern.

I look back, but the dog vanishes. One night I try to call Sophia, after agonizing over if I even should. I didn't want to hurt her more than I already did.

"Hey Sophia, I just wanted to say…"

"Can it wait? My dad's in the hospital…," she sniffles.

"OMG, is he ok?" I ask.

"We think so. His blood sugar was over three hundred, but he's still with us."

"Thank God! Okay, well, I just wanted to say I'm sorry. I can be kind of a jerk sometimes, and you didn't deserve that."

"It's ok, I know you have a lot of stress going on with school and now you're moving. But we can still talk, just not now. Mom's making me hang up. Love you, bye."

And the phone went dead.

"Well, at least she's not mad," I say to myself, as I return to staring at the ceiling.

The next night, squeaky wheels and sneakers come down the hallway before a nurse wheels someone new into my room. Her silvery-grey hair is matted like steel wool, and it looks like she's still in her long white nightgown from wherever she came from.

She raises her head, and I'm shocked by the glistening of her metallic silver eyes. "Mom? Is that you?" she asks.

"That's not your mom," says the orderly.

"Why are you bringing her here?" asks the nurse with the encrusted cubic zirconia glasses.

"We're out of rooms, and she's restless. And if she doesn't settle down, you guys know how to deal with it," he replies, throwing up his hands.

"Mom? Mom, is that you? Let her go! Let my mom go!" the girl spits.

The nurse with the glasses taps my shoulder.

"Hi, um, sweetie? Can you tell her that you aren't her mom?" she pleads.

"Sure," I say, hopeful that sleep will come for me if I could maybe calm her down.

3

DISCHARGED

I'm discharged after a couple of days and sent home armed with Klonopin for anxiety and Trazedone for sleep. My psychiatrist hesitates to prescribe anti-psychotics because of my age, but recommends constant monitoring as long as I'm on the drugs.

The first night, though, I stay with Tía Marisol and Tío Santos while Mom works an overnight shift. Tía Marisol worries herself with cleaning around the house, while Tío Santos is in the garage working on a project, and I take the time to sit semi-alone on the back patio.

The stormy sky is navy blue. Cars are whizzing along the freeway behind their fenced yard, and it's a cool fifty-six degrees. Too cold for crickets and their orchestra of strings, but it feels good to be outside. To relax... until the hairs on the back of my neck stand up, telling me I'm not alone anymore, and I whirl around to find the black on dark silhouette of a man standing in the doorframe.

"Tío Santos?" I whisper into the shadows.

An orange flame illuminates his skinny, paint-stained fingers as he lights the cigarette between his thin, taupe lips. He takes a drag, exposing the deep wrinkles carved by his sly grin and heavy moustache. He's only fifty, but he looks at least a decade older. Hard work, hard sun, and hard smoking takes a toll. His hands are his gift, he always says, slender, strong, and rough from his painting job and the odd jobs around the family houses.

"Don't tell your *Tía*. I told her I quit last week," he chuckles.

A smile creeps up my face.

"I'm no snitch," I say, smiling. "But you owe a secret back."

"Oh, so you *can* smile. You'd think that entire party would be enough to make anyone smile, but you're a tough customer," he says, grinning as if he won something.

"Well, not everything goes as planned," I say. "At least my mom got to show off in front of her friends... until the end. I guess it happens sometimes, when you throw an introvert a party."

"True, but she did it because she loves you, Selena. She is proud of you, mija. We're all proud of you," he says, leaning close to me.

Tío Santos was always a father figure, but usually the more silent kind. This is probably the longest conversation we've ever had, and it feels like he's really seeing me for me, whatever I am now.

"I know we don't talk much about your father, but he and I didn't make it past the fifth grade. You don't need a PhD like your mom or a trade like me to be worth something in this family. You just need to be you. Us Valencias are of strong stock. You know what Valencia means?"

"Strength," I say, finally smiling.

"Exacto. Your grandmother would always remind me of that," he says. "And strength means accepting sacrifice. So don't overthink too much, just live. Enjoy your youth, and strength will find you. It finds all of us Valencias. You're stronger than you think."

I sit, absorbing the time as it passes, as Tío and I grow silent with thought. And by the time Mom takes me home in the morning, she sorted plans for me to go stay with Tío Julio early, a month before she'll join us.

The heat of the next day is unbearable. I feel like a car running in the sun on our way to the airport for my flight to Tío Julio's. I roll down the window, and a blessedly cool breeze rushes in, cooling my skin, but not my mood. The meds worked on everyday stress, but this is not an everyday experience. My hair bounces like a cotton candy cloud as jets rumble through the sky when we finally exit the freeway.

Terminal 1:

Mom glides her gunmetal grey Corolla up to the curb at 'Departures' and pulls me into a hug that's almost as tight as my quinceañera corset.

"I'm going to miss you so, mija," Mom says. "But my brother is going to take good care of you, so I'll try not to worry."

Her hand cups my cheek. The spicy, floral scent of her perfume comforts me.

"I'm going to miss you, too, Mom, but don't worry. I'll be okay," I say, feeling bad after giving her such trouble, and even if I don't want to leave, I feel like she needs a break from me for a while.

"Call me as soon as you get there," she says, pointing at me as I make my way inside the sliding glass doors.

"Sure, Mamí," I say, holding back tears and wanting to get through the next month without any other surprises.

After a few hours on the plane, I collect my luggage at the whirring baggage claim and find a man fitting Tío's description by the 'Arrivals' exit. Tall, lanky, jeans, sunglasses, and baseball hat holding a sign with my name on it. He never used social media or sent any pictures of himself. I didn't understand how problematic that could be until now.

"Tío Julio?" I ask.

"Selena," he mutters in the monotone voice I remember from the phone calls he'd have with Mom.

The car ride home is awkward in the extreme. I haven't seen my uncle since I was a toddler, which means I never really talk to him except for, 'happy birthday.'

We make it to the farmhouse, and it is, as I expect, a small house on a big plot of land with a chicken coop, some sheep, cows and a few horses. Inside, the kitchen is plastered with decals of roosters the way the hall in our house is plastered with pictures of me.

"You sure must like roosters," I say, attempting to make conversation.

"Hmph," Tío grunts in response.

We sit in silence in a kitchen the size of my friend Sophia's walk-in closet. We surely aren't spoiled, my Tío is just… different.

"Not much of a conversationalist, are you?" I ask.

"No," he mutters.

"Cool, cool, cool, me neither," I say nervously.

Tío nods, settling into a still stare as he leans into his recliner chair.

"It's just that… I have a question," I say, to no response. "Is it true you're… you know?" I say, trying to hint.

"What, a monk?" he says, his eyebrows raised in an expectant way.

"No…," I say, falling off the proverbial cliff. "Gay?!" I say, almost whispering the exclamation. "I mean, you're in your late forties… no wife, no kids, or girlfriend."

"Yeah, I'm gay, is that a problem?" he says, now looking me dead in the eyes.

"No, it's cool. I've never really met an openly gay person before. You know, except for Rupaul's Drag Race. Have you seen it?" I ask, hoping to connect on something, because the farm is definitely something I can't relate to.

"Drag Race? No. But I've seen her perform live. She's majestic," he says, picking himself up and making his way to the refrigerator.

"Ah, so you can string a full sentence together. Prepositions and everything," I say, now sitting down at the kitchen table. Tío pulls a bottle of water out of the fridge and takes a sip.

"Hmph," he goes, again, tilting the bottle and looking at the water inside.

"We should watch it sometime," I suggest.

"Can't," he says, frowning at me. "No MTV or VH1." He wipes his mouth with his sleeve, and leans back against the sink.

"Well, I brought my laptop," I say enthusiastically, pulling my backpack off the chair.

"No Wi-Fi," he says, the sunlight from the window behind him makes him look darker in the dimness of the room.

"What? Are you kidding me? How do you live like this? What's your phone?" I say, now raising my voice. He pulls something small out of his pocket, and, as I feared, flips it open.

"Flip phone," he says, snapping it back shut.

"Mom said you're old fashioned, but she didn't say you're a *dinosaur*. I don't know if I can handle this. I need to go back home!" I say, feeling the room start to spin as my heartbeat kicks up its tempo. I need air, so I get up to head outside.

"Running from your problems. You definitely got that from the Valencia side of the family, because us Sol's don't run from our problems," he says, leaning over the small kitchen table.

"Excuse me," I say, leaning over my side of the table. "I haven't seen you since I was three years old. You don't get to drag me or my father like that," I continue, getting in his face. "And what are you doing out here, if not hiding from *your* problems?"

"You don't know what it's like," he says back, getting in my face, too. "You're spoiled and childish. I don't know why your mom thought it was a good idea to send you here. You aren't ready. You don't know what it's like to control yourself. To spend within your means. You don't even know what a hard day's work looks like."

My face is a furnace, pumping out warm, salty streams of tears down my cheeks. My lip quivers, and I let out a howl.

"What, what are you doing? Are you… are you crying?" Tío Julio asks, his forehead wrinkled with concern.

I suck in a lung full of air, the tears still running down my face.

"Isn't this what you wanted?" I wail even louder.

"How do I make it stop?" he says, verging on panic.

"You don't, I just need to let it out," I cry, and bury my head in my arms to cover my face.

"I'm calling your mother. I don't know how to handle this," he insists, and I hear him take out his flip phone and struggle to dial Mom's number.

"No se que hacer. We had a nice ride home, and then she complained about no Wi-Fi. I mentioned Arturo, and…."

"You did what!?" Mom barks through the speaker. "SHE'S STILL SENSITIVE ABOUT HER FATHER! AY, JULIO! PUT SELENA ON THE PHONE, NOW!"

"Ss-s-i-si hermana," Tío stammers.

"Mija," Mom says, her voice like a waterfall of calm. "I know it's not ideal. I know you miss me and your old life. But right now, you're not well. You have to learn from your uncle a different way of life. I can't take any more time off work to monitor you, and as rough around the edges as Julio is, he's a good man. He just doesn't know how to deal with teenagers. You don't want to hurt anyone, right? I need you to be brave and stay as long as you can. Until you learn to control your emotions, okay?" she says, her voice a soothing melody.

I wipe the tears rolling down my cheeks, "But Mom!"

"Mija, I know you don't like this arrangement, but you have to prove to me you can handle your emotions for at least a month. You need to show you can handle being by yourself without causing too much trouble. You're a woman now. Your sleep schedule has to get back to normal before you start school. You know I'm right."

"Fine," I say, biting my tongue, and genuinely wanting to do better, wanting to feel better.

"Good mija, give the phone back to Tío Julio, please."

"Here," I say, and Tío stares at the phone in fear. "Your turn again," I say, and he finally takes it back.

"Si?" he asks, turning to the farm field outside the kitchen window. "Mmm, hmmm, mmh, okay," he says, and takes his time closing his phone. I watch his unease through the dust floating in the air.

"I'll show you to your room," he finally says. "I have rules in this house, though. I should let you know before you get too comfortable."

"Perfect," I say sarcastically, feeling zero enthusiasm about his rules.

"Rule one," he says, turning to me and crossing his arms over his chest with a slack hip, making me imagine him stomping his cowboy boot down on the ground like a country pop star. "You eat what I serve you. Rule two…" he drones.

"Rule four…" I rest my chin on the edge of my palm.

"Are you listening? Selena, this is important."

"Yeah, yeah, I'm listening…" I say, perking up in my seat.

"…most important rule is curfew. It's sundown. Especially on a Full Moon. Girls have recently gone missing around here. Is that clear?"

"Sorry, I have a terrible attention span. Can you write this down?"

Tío groans, going out of sight down the hall. "Don't worry about it. I'll remind you in the morning. I'm going to bed. Good night."

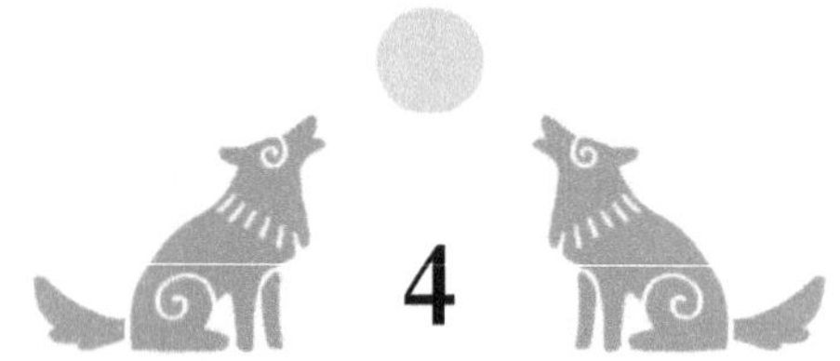

A PARTIAL HISTORY OF LA FAMILIA SOL-VALENCIA

"Wake up Selena, it's time for breakfast!" Tío says, knocking on my door.

I peer out from under the sheets and blankets, seeing only darkness out the window. "It's not even daylight out yet!" I argue.

"I need to feed you before you feed the chickens," Tío says.

"UGH!" I groan, getting out of bed before *he* gets more annoying. "Can you at least make coffee and something edible?" I ask as I change out of my pajamas.

"Sure, now set the table when you get in here," he says, before clunking down the hall to the kitchen.

In the kitchen, I go for the mugs first and set them on the table. "Where's the plates?" I ask, not seeing any in the cabinets or shelves that fit between the sink and stove where Tío's cooking... something.

"Under the sink," he says, pouring himself some... tea?

"But these are paper plates," I say, picking one up and bending it.

"They work just fine," he says, snatching it out of my hand and setting it on the table.

"And they're terrible for the environment, farm boy. I thought you were a sustainable farmer," I say, leaning against the sink. "Do you use plastic forks and knives, too?"

"Listen, I live alone," he says, opening the cabinet over the stove and pulling out a box of shaky cutlery before slamming it next to me for effect. "I'd rather not spend my free time washing dishes," he says.

"Well, that's silly. You could just get a dishwasher."

"It's not the same… Why do I even have to justify this? Will you just set the table?!" he barks.

"Fine," I say, and I finish setting everything out. "Mom's going to have a lot more to say when she gets here. She might even have more rules than you."

"My sister always has a lot to say," Tío Julio says, pouring me coffee in the slowest way, letting it gurgle into my mug. "She had a lot to say about your *party*, too." And I could feel the weight of the coffee as he poured. "Coffee for you. Your ma' said you'd like it. I drink Earl Grey. You should, too. It's not a rule, but it's pretty close to one. You'll find out soon enough. Aren't you a little young for coffee, anyway?" he asks.

"I started drinking coffee when I started high school. I had to wake up early so I could make the bus on time," I say, adding way too much... milk.

"All those cows and no creamer?" I ask, trying not to sound annoyed. "And yes, my party was a disaster. But my psychiatrist advised me not to talk about it."

"I might be the last small farmer supplying the grocery outlet with cream, but I'm not going anywhere or ruining that contract. If you want creamer, you go get it yourself. Down at the store. I'll need you to go later for things. And if you change your mind about talking, I'm here. Sometimes it's good to let it out. Us Sols, you included of course, are passionate. Around here, people are reserved. We might be loud and clash about things, but that's how we figure things out. Around the Full Moon you might change your mind about the coffee," he says, stirring his tea and blowing on it. "You'll be changing, and it's going to get you *so* wired. You have no idea."

"I know how periods work," I say, choosing *not* to talk about the party or *anything* that happened at it. The shadowy wolf figure included. I can still sense it, but can't feed into it.

"You need to hear me out, Selena," Tío Julio says. "Our family history... Your family history is important. You need to learn a lot of what I have to teach you if you want to be prepared for being a full grown... Sol-Valencia. Do you know anything about your family history? Has your mom told you anything?" he asks.

"No, I don't think so," I say, hoping he'll stop. "I know she got her period late, too, but not this late."

"What? Periods?" Tío Julio says, looking derailed.

Please lose track. Please let me go.

"Maybe it isn't my place to talk about with you..."

"Wait, what do you mean?" I ask, sipping my cafecito, maybe half-hoping he'd tell me about my were-girl gift? Curse? Probably more of a curse. "And what are these?" I complain, poking at the pinkish-pale blobs he set down on the plate in front of me, unsure of how much pressure I'd need to burst them open for their yellow goop to flow out.

"Eggs Benedict with vegan bacon," he sighs.

"Gross, I don't eat benedict eggs."

Tío Julio clears his throat.

"What?" I ask.

"Rule one," he says, tapping his temple with a finger.

"What is it, again?" I ask.

"You eat what I serve you. This isn't 'Burger Queen.' You can't 'have it your way.' We eat what we raise and kill on the farm, and pork substitutes," he says, cutting his vegan bacon with a knife and fork before putting a small bite into his mouth.

"Why can't we eat pork again?" I ask, really hoping not to offend him. But his face grows a peony pink as he loses patience.

"Listen, over the years, I've compiled a list of rules that have worked for me in managing my... emotions and anger, and they've worked to keep everyone safe. I haven't killed, attacked, or maimed anyone in a long time," he says, counting his fingers.

"Well, that's a pretty good track record for a would-be serial killer," I say, starting to see Tío Julio's ambitions as a lot lower than I'd thought. Maybe a lot lower than I'd hoped for for my life, too. I never thought of adults struggling to just *live*. Even when they seem to have themselves figured out.

"If you want to do things your way and risk your life, be my guest. Don't come to me for help and then complain when I give it to you," he says, pointing his fork at me.

"Tell me then," I say, now staring *him* in the eyes. "All you have to tell me, tell me now."

"Fine," he says. "I can't say all I have to tell you, but I can start." Tío Julio swallows another bit of eggs and bacon, and washes it down with Earl Grey, then meets me again with his eyes to show me he's ready.

"There hasn't always been a division between our tribes, the Valencias and the Sols. United, we used to be two of the most powerful families, before we were divided by governments, treatises and borders," Tío Julio says. "Ever since the Treaty of Guadalupe, we've been divided. We are the North of the border werewolves, and there are South of the border werewolves, and our greatest strengths became our greatest weaknesses. The schism of that land purchase stripped us of so much of our power.

South of the border families live and hunt in packs. They're communal. That was always their specialty, but that means they're tied to the land, too. They don't do well away from our ancestral lands, and they don't migrate easily. North of the border werewolves are more solitary, like me, for example. We used to live on the outskirts of the community, solo hunting and scouting, and... would go on other missions. I don't hunt alone, though, or with anyone else. I don't eat meat. I've, effectively, kept the worst of my instincts in remission with the rules I'll teach you. You need to learn this control regardless of if you want to or not. They're going to be the only things that keep you from harming yourself or others, again. You want to talk about the party?"

When it's my turn to talk, I realize I've been swishing the same sip of coffee I took when he started his monologue, and it takes conscious effort to swallow. Tío Julio's right, I don't need the energy. I'm already wired, but it's hard for me to process everything around my past coming to life in a way I can't even imagine.

"I'm sorry, werewolves? Schism? Aren't we human?"

"We don't have time for this now, Selena. Eat, get through your denial. And think about what I said. You need to feed the chickens, and I need to feed the cows."

"Fine," I say, thinking more about how disgusting his eggs are than about the fact that, yes, I guess, I *am* a werewolf. Which, I think, are also humans, as well as whatever I turned into at my party.

I shove a forkful of whatever was on my plate into my mouth without looking at it, and actually enjoy the flavors in a way I didn't expect my tongue to like. I devoured everything but the plate, my hunger driving me more than anything else.

When I'm ready, I clean up and put on the black cowgirl boots my mom gave me before she actually let me know we were moving to Vacaville. At least that made sense looking back. As for my family history, it was hard to think about in the midst of figuring out my new, hopefully temporary, home and life.

"Do they have names?" I ask Tío, as I follow him out the back door and out onto the farm.

"Names? Why would they have names? They're just chickens," he says laughing.

"Then, can I name them?"

"Sure, just don't get distracted. They get vicious if you don't feed them on time," he jokes. "Maybe that could be one of their names. Vicious."

"I'll see," I say, opening the chicken coop as tío walks off for the cows in the fields. As soon as I lift open the coop door, several chickens walk out into the range, clucking happily as I feed them grains and corn from the bucket.

"Let me see," I say to them. "You'll be Carla. Now, you look more like Juanita to me. You're definitely Brandy…" I go on and name the rest. Twenty-seven in total, if I didn't mix them up.

After a bit, I see Tío Julio heading back towards the house, and I decide my time with the chickens is enough.

"You have a learners permit, right?" he asks, coming up to the chicken range.

"Yeah," I say, unsure if he was serious about sending me to the store.

"I need you to go into town. The Safeway should have the bread we need. We also need cereal and some veggies I don't grow. There's a list on the fridge. Do you think you can handle that?" he says, handing me the keys to his pickup.

"I'm not supposed to drive without a licensed adult," I sigh, actually nervous about driving his old truck. My mind's different now, more distracted, more active, less focused, even if I felt more intense and on edge than usual.

"Trust me, it's better I'm not with you when you're driving. My nerves make it worse," he says, rubbing his temples.

"You have anxiety, too?" I ask.

"With being in the car with others, especially," Tío Julio says. "Ever since I hit that pole. Why you think I didn't say much on the ride from the airport?"

"Oh, wow," I say. "My psychiatrist said I have severe anxiety. I guess it runs in the family, too. I heard about the pole. Your story is why I take driving so seriously."

He pats my back, but doesn't say anything back.

"Drive carefully," he finally says. "I don't want to have to deal with your mother if something happens to you. I love her, and I love you. I promised her. That means don't talk to strangers. That's a rule. Keep a low profile, another rule. I don't need anyone gossiping about us, you hear? That's a rule."

He unclips the glasses on his shirt neck and slides them onto his face. Then stares at me with a high brow to tell me he isn't moving until he gets the answer he wants.

"Fine," I say, forgetting the rules, and more focused on his performance. He could be an actor, the way he moves his body.

"Good. Call me, if anything," he says, holding up his flip phone and heading back to the fields.

The white pickup truck is cleaner than I'd expect for an old farm truck. Tío doesn't have much, but he takes care of what he has, that's for sure. And I'm grateful to be headed into town, especially being the only one on the road. In both directions.

The Safeway parking lot is empty except for a few cars, and I make sure to grab the reusable bags on the passenger seat before I get out, even if I forgot to grab the list after I looked at it. Inside, I head directly for the produce, and start inspecting every fruit and vegetable before deciding on it. Every bruise, mold speck, and defect I find, I'm led by… sniffing it out before I see it.

"You're new in town," I hear, in a deep voice behind me.

He's a tall, lanky, and tan Vietnamese guy. A little bit older looking than fifteen, but definitely around my age.

"What's it to you?" I say back to him, returning to my vegetables. He's cute, but I don't want to let on that I think so.

"Nothing, just trying to be friendly is all. My name's Caleb, and your name?" he says, leaning against the edge of the cabbage display.

"I don't plan to reveal it, if that's what you're waiting for," I say, moving to inspect a cabbage.

"Mystery Girl, it is. Well, I'll see you around, I guess. Oh, just be careful. A girl from my class went missing last week. You actually look like her a bit."

"Thanks for the concern? I don't stay out long," I say, weirded out a little.

"If you need any help, I'll be stocking the canned food in aisle seven," he says, and smiles before turning out of sight.

"Thanks," I say to myself, happy he's gone. The less I have to tell Tío Julio, the better.

After I finish with the produce, I head for the bakery. But I'm not alone in the aisle. And as my hand reaches for the last loaf of my favorite bread, someone else's hand brushes against mine.

"Oh, I'm sorry!" the girl whispers. She looks about my age, too. Tall, pale, with long curly brown hair and glasses.

"It's okay, you can have it," she says, raising her hands in surrender.

"Thanks," I smile, holding back a growl that almost slipped out from the fright.

"My name's Daisy," she says, disarming my suspicion of her with a stretched out hand.

"Cute bracelet," I say, reaching to shake, but the tips of my fingers light up in pain the closer I get, until...

"Ouch!" I flinch from the pain, feeling genuinely burned from her touch.

"Come with me," Daisy gasps, pulling me toward the bathroom with her *other* hand.

"What are you doing?" I ask, nearly tripping over her feet.

"Shhh... I didn't want to ask you this out in the open," she whispers, "but how long have you been a werewolf?"

"Wait, what?" I ask, disbelieving she could ask me such a thing.

'I'm not your mom,' I want to tell her, to maybe snap her out of whatever psychotic episode she's having, but she's right.

"Selena?" she asks.

"How do you know my name?" I answer back. "What is it with small towns that makes people feel entitled to pop into other peoples' lives, as if people *want* to be bothered?" And I finally pull my arm loose from her grasp.

"Are you out of your mind?" Daisy asks.

I stop in my tracks.

"Excuse me?" I say, wondering if I heard her right.

"Don't worry, I won't tell anybody. My mom's one too. Fortunately, I'm adopted," she explains, and I feel more lost than a toddler in a carnival maze.

"That's great, Daisy, but, um, why do you think I'm a werewolf…?" I say, still not quite following. Just because she's right, doesn't mean I'm letting her win the argument.

"Your reaction to the silver. It's one-hundred percent pure. My mom got it for me for protection," she says, stroking the shining silver links of her bracelet.

"Well, this is awkward, then," I say. "I don't know how to tell you this, but I'm not a werewolf. There must be something in the water here, because werewolves don't exist. I've only ever had peaceful, calm Full Moons to look back on, and I think that's a good indicator," I sigh, hoping that's good enough.

"Oh, so you're a late bloomer! My mom was, too," she says.

"I'm not talking about my period!" I say. "Are *you* out of *your* mind?" I ask.

"You can trust me," she says, pleading at me like my mom. "After all, didn't I confront you privately? If I wanted to make a scene, I could have. Plus, we're friends now!"

She finishes every sentence with more enthusiasm every time she opens her mouth, and it's making my head spin.

"I can't be friends with you," I say. "I'm only in town for the day. I'm heading back to the farm after this, for, I don't know how long."

"Pretty much everyone from town lives on a farm," she says. "That makes us neighbors, not strangers! We can't escape each other even if we tried, and school's just around the corner. We're going to see each other all the time. Let's get some ice cream and have some fun."

"I'm watching my sugar," I sigh, looking for an excuse my mom would use and feigning disappointment.

"Well, I'm out of tries for the day, I guess. Take my number if you change your mind about hanging out," Daisy says with a smile, handing me a... business card.

"Do all teenagers have business cards around here?" I ask, feeling more out of place in ways I never expected.

"Successful ones!" she says. "I'm the busiest babysitter in town. I'm also a dog walker too, but that's my side hustle."

"Well, it's nice to meet you, Daisy," I say, and slide her card into my back pocket.

"I'm a professional dog sitter, too," she says as she brushes past me. "If you ever need one."

She continues out of the ladies room, but I take a second to hold back. It feels weird that she knew, and even weirder that I still feel watched. By the black dog I keep seeing, or... something else.

I finish my shopping with more purpose than before, probably feeling more the way my uncle does when he visits town. It sucks getting attention when all you want to be is invisible. That would be a more welcome curse, I guess.

After I somehow remember everything Tío Julio listed and pick up a bottle of the creamer with Tío Julio's face on it, I make for the checkout line. And as I set everything down, the cashier steps out to go on break.

"We've gotta stop meeting like this," I hear where the cashier was just replaced.

It's the Caleb kid, with a big cheeky smile on his face.

"Oh great, my first stalker," I say, shooting him a quick and serious glance. Maybe my most menacing, and flirty, glance yet.

"I don't know if you've noticed, but I work here. So, it kinda looks like you're stalking me," he teases back.

"Well, I'll be happy if we never run into each other again," I say, rolling my eyes. For some guys, being hurtful is the only way you're taken seriously.

"That's harsh," he says, starting to scan my items.

"I'm just messing with you," I say. "I'm in an awkward situation right now, and it's just a lot in my head all the time."

I rummage for the cash in my wallet that Mom gave me to 'help out with things.' But I can buy and buy and buy, and the house would still need stuff. Tío Julio has his work cut out for him as a one-man farm.

"Yeah, it gets that way," Caleb says, waving the options in the air like a magician. "Paper or plastic?"

"Oh, I brought my own bags," I say, pulling them out of the tote I stuffed them in.

"Ay, si, mami! We love an environmentally conscious cowgirl queen," a rather flamboyant teenager wearing a collection of patterns and colors snaps behind me. "You rockin' them boots, hunny."

"Bye," I say abruptly to both of them as Caleb hands me the change. "I appreciate the compliments, though. Now watch me walk out that door and never come back."

"You'll be back next week, at least, Mystery Girl," Caleb hollers, and I keep walking without looking back.

"You go cowgirl!" the flamboyant teen in the peacock outfit shouts, and I wish I'd met him before the other two. I might have actually left with a friend I could have fun with and who seems to already be my biggest fan.

By the time I find the road back to Tío Julio's, my stomach is groaning like a hungry dog, even though it's only a couple of hours since breakfast. My appetite's crazy. I'm not sure if it's the meds or what, but, honestly, I'm not sure if I should even be driving with what I'm on.

5

IN THE HEART OF THE WOLF'S DEN

"Wait for me!" I hear over the drone of the truck engine and clamour of the bleating sheep herd crossing the dusty road and keeping me from Tío Julio's house. Hot, sticky air filters in through the open windows, and behind me a woman is chasing after a few stray, leaping sheep. The sheep, doing everything they can to stay away from the fluffy white dog, rejoin the herd, and the woman reins in the dog's leash as they reach the roadside.

"You've got to be kidding me," I laugh, surprised to see anyone pop out of the fields, let alone a woman with a shampoo-commercial-perfect strawberry-blonde bob that bounces in slow motion.

"Sorry 'bout this!" she shouts, making her way to the driver's window. "I haven't seen your face before," she says, wiping the sweat off her forehead.

"Yeah," I say, suspicious of her, even if she appears comfortable with me.

"I recognized the truck. You know Julio doesn't get out much? I was hoping to say hello. It's a real shame," she says, pulling off her gloves. "But it's nice to meet someone else in the family. I'm Shirley, what's your name?"

She holds out her hand. No silver bracelet, so I shake.

"Selena. It's nice to meet you, too," I say. "My tío doesn't say much, even when around. He's a private person."

"Especially lately. I haven't seen him since my sheep started going missing. Well, you tell him I say hello and that he doesn't have to be a stranger if he doesn't want to be! We're family here in Vacaville."

"I'll tell him you said hello," I say, thanking the sheep as they fully cross the road, opening up my way home.

"Thank you, doll," Shirley says, with a smile warm enough to melt butter. "You take care now."

"Bye," I say, hoping Tío Julio isn't wondering where I am.

"I'm back!" I shout, carrying the groceries inside the house.

"I thought I told you not to talk to anyone. You had one job: go into town to get bread and stuff. Instead, you socialize with a neighbor who's on a need-to-know basis about my business?" Tío says, flailing his arms as he paces the kitchen.

"What do you mean?" I ask, unsure of how he could possibly know anything about who I talked to, unless gossip travels around small towns faster than I could even imagine.

"I heard you talking to nosy Shirley. She doesn't need to know a damn thing about my life," he says. "She needs to keep herself and assumptions far away from here."

"But that was at least a half-mile away, you honestly expect me to believe you could hear what we were saying?" I squeak, shifting my feet.

"I heard perfectly clear," he growls.

"So, what? I'm just supposed to be completely isolated here?!" I say, raising my voice, too.

"More or less, yes! We don't know what you are yet. You could put others in danger or, worse, us in danger. Do you know what they do to people who are different in this pueblo? Especially if they see us as a threat? We won't last long," he says, his voice getting loud. I recognize the fear, or anxiety in him that controls me sometimes, too.

"I'm so sick of this already! It's 2010, nobody cares if you're gay. I'm going to my room," I say, not wanting to talk about my werewolf scare at the grocery store.

I know what I am, and I don't need my tío, mom, or psychiatrists to tell me who I am. I don't care if neighbors who pretend to care, hate me. I just want to have fun, like any other kid. It doesn't matter that I had my quinceañera, especially if I'm trapped on a farm in the middle of Vacaville.

Nothing actually matters, except getting out of here. Because, until then, I'm nothing. I don't know if I'm more Valencia or more Sol, but I'm starting to feel like I don't really fit in anywhere. And that feels... okay to me. Drama queen, Tío Julio is just going to have to deal with it!

In my back pocket, I find the pokey business card from Daisy, and wonder if I should call her. Sophia's busy with her dad, and Mom's at work at this time, but I need to talk to *someone* to get my mind off things. And Tío Julio probably doesn't even know Daisy's from town. She also just might have some answers for me to show Tío Julio I can, in fact, handle myself.

"Daisy's Babysitting, Dogsitting, Dogwalking Services Incorporated, how may I help you?" she answers.

"Hey," I whisper, worried about Tío hearing.

"Selena?" she asks.

"How did you know?" I say.

"I know everyone in this town, and your number is about the only one I don't recognize by heart," she says.

"Oh," I say. "Well, I need to get off this farm."

"That's what all the girls in this town say," she says.

"I just feel like the cards I was dealt are, like, totally unfair compared to everyone else's," I say, laying back on my pillows the way I used to when Sophia and I would talk for hours.

"No matter what," Daisy says. "It's like my mom always says. There's always someone who has it easier and harder than you do. She's not wrong about a lot."

"I guess that's true," I say. "God, I miss my mom so much. I miss my friend Sophia, and my old way of life. I wish I could just blink and have everything back the way it was. Before my quinceañera. Before the were-I called home changed," I sigh, crumbling over the weight of my near slip up.

"Your were-... wolf transformation?" Daisy digs.

"This again?" I ask, playing it off.

"Well, either way, I'm sorry you feel bad about being here. Nothing interesting ever happens here. Except for..." she trails off.

"Except for what?" I say, straightening up, intrigued.

"Well, a girl went missing last week. They're still investigating. We even have a curfew because of it," she whispers. "I think it was werewolves."

"That Caleb kid said something about that. You think it was werewolves, or you *know* it was werewolves?" I ask, full of accusation. The way she kept accusing me.

"What are you really asking?" she says faintly.

"Was it your parents?" I say.

"No, of course not. Mom was chained up in the basement that night," she says confidently.

"Well, that's horrifying! But good, I guess. In a twisted kind of way. At least you know it wasn't her. Do they have any other leads?" I ask.

"Well, it's more than just one girl. *Several* girls in the *region* have been missing lately. No unusual characters have been around, and the police don't know where to turn. But there were pawprints. No dogs have been missing, but there've been sightings of wolves all season. This was just the first girl from our town. If I were you, even if you are a werewolf, you need to be careful if you go out at night," she says, her voice trembling.

"Are there a lot of werewolves in the area?" I ask.

"I don't know everything," she says. "My mom keeps most stuff away from me. That's why I do all this research to stay on top of everything, so that I know what I'm doing if my parents are the ones who don't come home one day."

"Wow, that's deep," I say. "I never thought about that back home. My mom's always been the strongest thing I've ever known in the universe. She always says I have it easier than she did, and I thank her, because I'm not made for life out here. I'm the chicken feeder here. I'm only able to even have this conversation because of the meds I'm on. I'm not ready for all this."

"The meds you're on?" Daisy says. "That explains it! You need to embrace the wolfgirl inside of you. Get rid of those things! My mom takes something before she chains herself up. She says a lot of people are born with gifts not made for our world today, and how people cover up their gifts by countering the chemicals inside their bodies. It has its time and place, definitely. And it helps a lot of people, but it might be keeping you more human for now. For now, I think you need to learn to navigate this world as a werewolf before you hide from this part of yourself forever. You can master this."

"You're saying a lot of stuff that sounds very... out there, Daisy. So, forgive me. Don't get too comfortable in my business. I might be more friendly than my Tío, but I don't want to be open about these things with you to that level."

"The more human blood you spill, even if you lose control and even if it's in self-defense, the more powerful and wild you'll become. The more wild you become, the more empathy you'll lose for human life. If you don't master this, you'll lose yourself to it. That's what I'm afraid we're dealing with out there... A wild-werewolf. Not rabid, but not tamed. Lost behind the lobo..."

"Hold on, I think my uncle's at the door. I want to finish this conversation. I'll call you later," I say, hanging up the phone as Tío opens the door. Maybe I have super hearing, too.

"It's customary to knock before entering a woman's bedroom," I say in the serious way my mom often says things like that.

"Geez, you sound just like my sister," Tío Julio says, looking at the ceiling before closing the door between us. "You good now?"

"Come in," I say, wondering what he actually wants.

"I want to apologize," he says, settling himself at the foot of my bed. "I listened to some music to calm down. That's another rule, if you want to write it down."

"I got it," I say. "Go on."

"I know you feel I'm too strict, but the rules I set are strict for a reason. I warned you before: exposure could trigger an unpredictable and possibly violent reaction. There are girls in this region around your age who have gone missing. I promised your mother I would protect you, and I intend to keep my promise," he says, eyes filled with sadness.

I wait for a beat or two.

"Okay, apology accepted, and I'll try to be better about following the rules. But I need some flexibility here," I say, willing to compromise if I can't beat him.

"I'm sure we can find middle ground. When you're ready, please come to the kitchen. I have a few surprises for you."

In the kitchen, I find a tres leches cake with a jewelry box sitting beside it.

"What's this for?" I ask, excited about something other than chickens for the first time all day.

"Since I couldn't be there for your quinceañera, I said to myself, 'she deserves a tres leches cake.' But the jewelry box and what's inside of it are your mother's. She wanted to give it to you the night of your quinceañera, but she didn't have time since you were in the hospital."

He stands back, waiting for me to open it, but the box itself is a beautiful dark wood, with a perfect ruby red half-sphere that reflects the light in its center.

Inside the jewelry box is an ornate, gold cross necklace with a ruby in the center of the crucifix.

"It's beautiful," I sigh.

Tío clasps the necklace around my neck, and my mom's love floods me as if she were there in the room with us.

6

A DAY WITH DAISY

I awake again to the sound of Tío cooking breakfast. The sizzle of the pan and alluring smell of Mexican seasonings make my mouth water, and I'm drooling...

I set the table and tend to the chickens without Tío asking, my hunger driving me on autopilot. I never remembered to call Daisy back before falling asleep, but I hope to, if Tío decides to drown his feelings in music again. I still need my conversations to be private, even if he's going to try to meet me half way on things.

After I finish up outside, I wash my hands and take a seat at the table while Tío brings the food over for us.

"So, I didn't actually listen to music last night to calm down," he says, filling my plate with eggs, soyrizo, and white rice. My mouth's watering, but it sounds like Tío might be on his way to ruining another meal together. Though, it's a plus that this one looks edible. "I overheard your conversation with your friend," he continues.

"Shit," I slip.

"There's not much you can hide from me. You're just going to have to face it."

"Okay," I say. "She found me in the grocery store. She called me out after I flinched at her *pure silver* bracelet. There's not much I could've done. I denied it. I still deny it, honestly."

"I heard that, too," Tío says, holding up a hand. "I had a conversation on the phone with your mom. You're not in trouble. You can go out with your friend today if you want, but try not to break any more rules," he says, and sips the tea from his mug.

"Really?! Are you sure?" I ask, feeling so revved up by the news that coffee sounds like too much to handle.

"I'm sure, but I insist on meeting her. I need to know if we can trust her, and I'd like to meet at least one of her parents," he says, tapping his foot. "That's non-negotiable."

"Deal," I say, wondering what malls around Vacaville even look like.

After breakfast I call Daisy and ask if her mom would drive us to go shopping, and they're both on board.

"Be back by 6," Tío says, as Daisy and I figure out plans on the phone.

"9," I say back.

"7:30," he says.

"Deal!" I shout, excited with Daisy on the other end. Maybe it's the chickens, or the endless fields of grass, but I need to be around sleek tiled floors, clothing racks, and discount signs, bad.

"Well, well, well, if it isn't Julio Sol," says Daisy's mom as she walks around her white Suburban and up to Tío Julio and I. She's a lot shorter than Daisy, with a straight bob and is petite and dainty in how she holds up her hands. I don't know what I expected from a were-mom, but she definitely isn't it. "Amelia Vazquez, so nice to meet you both."

Tío Julio shakes her outstretched hand and smiles at her with amusement.

"It's nice to meet you, too," he says. "It's nice of Daisy and yourself to take Selena on a girls day. I was afraid she'd have trouble making friends, being so far out on the farm and all."

"Well, not much passes by my Daisy without her *getting in the know*," Amelia says. "It's a pleasure for us that Daisy's made a new friend. And, well, I haven't been out this way in ages. You gotta make it to town more often, Julio. The town needs a little bit of coming together. Especially now."

"Yeah, I heard about the missing girls from the area on the radio. I was afraid to bring Selena out here because of it."

"You're smart for worrying," she says. "I've been worried, too. My husband is more in the know on all that. He's been joining the men on the search parties... You'll have to join us one night for dinner, and we can all get to know each other a little more. I've got some errands to run with the girls, so let's talk more soon."

"Let's exchange numbers, so you can reach me if anything happens," Tío says, turning Amelia back around. "I'll be in the fields with the cows for a while today. Selena's curfew is 7:30. Nice meeting you, Amelia, Daisy. Selena, be safe and have fun. I'm still getting used to having another person around to watch over."

"Well, you're definitely doing right by her," Amelia says. "Here's my business card. Leave me a voicemail, and I'll know it's you."

"Thanks, Tío," I say, watching him take the business card that I notice looks similar to Daisy's. Then, I follow Daisy to the rear door of the SUV, half expecting to see a box of personalized business cards on the seat with my information on it. Luckily, nothing's there.

"Take care, Julio," Amelia says. "See you later!"

"Bye, Julio!" Daisy says, smiling at him as we get in.

At the mall, Amelia drops us off at the food court. It's not as nice as the mall in Santa Ana, but it's definitely better than cow fields. Even if it feels like stepping back into the... I don't even know what decade brought us bright red booths, brown walls, and puke green flooring.

"Why don't I go grab that table over there?" Daisy says, pointing to the only table open in the mediocre court. A few kids were running around with their moms sitting amongst the mall workers and between the elderly munching on early bird bucket deals. And the line for the Indian restaurant is the longest, which is where we're at. "It looks like we'll be eating on the floor, unless you want to go for it?"

"No, that's okay," I say "I'm still deciding what I want. Text me your order."

After a minute of thinking everything sounds too good to not order, the line behind me starts to grow, and someone gets so close I have to turn around from his breath on my neck.

"Can I help you?" I ask. It's a boy, my age, handsome, but overall just a gawky white guy squinting up at the menu.

"Sure, I'm trying to read the menu, but I lost my glasses. And my friend ditched me to go talk to some girl. Would you mind reading me the menu?"

"Sure," I say. "Most people in the city would just take a picture with their phone and zoom in, but creeping up people's necks works too, I guess."

"I'm so sorry," he says, getting red and covering his mouth with his hand in embarrassment. "I didn't realize I was breathing on you. I honestly just kept walking, trying to read."

"It's fine," I say, and we contemplate the menu options and decide on the same thing, Chicken Tikka Masala. A classic.

"What's your name?" I ask him, enjoying his friendliness.

"Jonathan, but you can call me John," he says. "And you?"

"Selena, call me Selena, and I don't want to see you eat alone, on the floor. My friend and I got the last table, so you might want to join us."

"Well, I wouldn't want to intrude," he says, shaking his head. "But I'd really rather not eat on the floor more, so sure. I'll join."

"Cool," I say, hoping he's trying to be sweet. "I'm sure my friend won't mind," I tell him, really hoping she won't.

When we get close, Daisy gives me a screwy look.

'What?' I mouth at her, and she just throws her hands up in the air in surrender.

"So, ladies, what are your plans?" John asks after we sit down.

"Honestly, I'm not sure. I thought we were just going to people-watch. Maybe catch a movie," I reply. "I could *look* at clothes, but I feel like it might not be worth it out here."

"My mom orders all our stuff online for us," Daisy says, digging into her curry. "It's not terrible out here, but definitely slower on the fashion side."

"What movie were you thinking of seeing?" John asks, his lips thick with sauce as his face reddens from the spice.

"It's a chick flick, you probably wouldn't be into it," Daisy says, jumping in.

"Oh," he says, looking down.

"I was also thinking a thriller might be nice, though," I say, swallowing hard, and wanting to kick Daisy under the table.

There's something about him that makes me not want to leave him alone. Maybe the loneliness in his eyes.

"Fine," Daisy says, giving up with crossed arms. Her and Sophia are very different, but they both have a fire in them that makes me almost want to laugh.

"Thank you," I whisper to her, and grab her arm. Why not be distracted a *little* more?

"What's your favorite elective this year?" I ask him, curious about his interests.

"Um... English. Specifically, 18th Century Literature," he says.

"Oh, impressive" I say. "I like the British classics. I've finished Sense and Sensibility, at least. That's gotta be a tough elective, though."

"Yeah, it is," he says. "But I'm good at reading... up close at least." And we both laugh, further annoying Daisy from the look in her eye.

"He couldn't read the menu, that's how we started talking. He lost his glasses," I say to her.

"Charming," she adds. "You mean, the glasses sticking out of the plant over there?"

"Where?" he asks, whipping around to look behind us.

"Oh, I'll grab them," I say, seeing them sticking out of a fake olive bush along the divider wall ledge. "Try them out," I say, lowering them onto the bridge of his nose.

"These are them," he says. "Left-of-center scratch and everything!"

"Now you can *really* come with us to the movie," I say, glancing at Daisy.

"Oh yeah," John says, laughing. "I didn't even realize I wouldn't be able to see. Thanks for finding my glasses," he tells Daisy. "Popcorn on me."

"Sounds like a plan," I say, actually feeling... happy?

"This is cool," I say to Daisy, watching John walk off for the popcorn line.

"I can't believe you invited him!" Daisy hisses.

"What's wrong?" I ask, surprised with her. She seemed so bubbly before.

"There's just something about him I don't like. He's a privileged know-it-all. His family owns the largest farm in Vacaville, and I hear they're *real* conservative, too."

"Let's just give him a chance. He seems nice enough," I say.

"I saw the way you were looking at him. You're crushing hard," she says in a rough way. "It's written all over your face."

"I just think we should give him a chance," I say, kind of feeling like she's a little right.

"You can't lie to me. I work with children all the time who try to get away with mistruths," she says, crossing her arms again, and it feels like having Sophia back with me.

"Do you work as a nanny, or for the FBI?" I ask with a smirk, impressed with her stubbornness. "Let's get our seats, and he can meet us."

"Alright," Daisy says. "And I might just work for both."

"Hopefully your experience doesn't have to come in handy," I say, hoping with every fiber in my body that my body won't betray me now.

We get seats in the middle of the theatre, my favorite spot. Daisy's on my left, and John sits on my right when he finds us with a big bucket of popcorn in hands.

After the trailers, his fingers slip between mine, and start to feel hot and anxious. In a way I only felt the night of my quinceañera. I turn to him, but he acts like he doesn't see me. I want to scream! I'm *so* not used to getting attention from guys, and quickly my whole body blossoms with heat to the point that my forehead feels like it could fry an egg.

"Geez, is it hot in here?" I say, pulling at my hoodie.

"Are you kidding me, it's freezing?" Daisy whispers.

"Are you okay?" John asks me, pulling my hand closer to him and out of sight of Daisy.

"Yeah. Yeah, I'm fine," I say, trying to settle down, but I can't lean my head against his head when he puts it on my shoulder. I'd just about burst out in flames.

Before the movie even starts, my nails start bulging out of their beds, feeling pulled out of my skin and bone. And in the second after I rip my hand from John's, both of my hands transform into claws, thankfully still hidden by the darkness.

"I need to pee," I squeak, and I squeeze past Daisy, running out of the theatre as fast as I can.

What feels like ages later, I make it to an empty stall as the rest of my body burns with a pain that *does* make me scream. A silent whisper of a scream, as I wheeze for breath. The cold stall door against my forehead, the struggle of my hyperventilating lungs. My... claws.

"What the actual fuck?" I shout, looking down at them, opening and closing them through the pain of the sore, bulging muscles. "How am I turning *now*?" I ask myself, wanting to slam my body against the walls of the stall to make it stop.

Then the bathroom door opens, and Daisy's red TOMS pad their way to the other side of my stall door.

"Are you alright? ¿Estas bien?" Daisy asks, in the gentlest way.

I open the stall door, and we both gasp. Her out of shock, and me out of pure, cry-worthy desperation.

"Now, this I've never seen before," she says.

"I'm freaking out here!" I say, struggling to breathe through the knives stabbing in my chest.

"Let me call my mom, she'll know what to do," she says.

"Hold me," I say, falling into her arms, and sobbing against her shoulder.

When Daisy's mom arrives, she advises me to think peaceful thoughts and take deep breaths.

"This is one of the unfortunate symptoms of late blooming," Amelia says. "Instead of it coming all at once, it comes in trickles. Until you can control it, at least. Is Julio teaching you? I won't tell him we had this conversation."

She's kind, and calming, in a way that surprises me for an undercover, functioning were-mom. She's patient with me as I focus on my breath, now sitting on the throne of the stall. As my temperature cools, my claws start to retract back to normal fingers, and I don't know how much time's passed.

At one point, a lady walks in to wash her hands at the sink, and looks back at us in the mirror. Can't blame her for staring. I would, too.

"Is everything alright?" she asks, out of concern or judgment I'm not sure.

"Cramps," Daisy says, not missing a beat to craft a narrative, and the woman leaves us back to our conversation. But my mind is too fast to catch onto a thought.

After the paw incident, Daisy's mom drives us back to Tío's, and Daisy walks me to the front door.

"Thanks for spending time with me. Sorry it got weird," Daisy says. "It can happen to new werewolves. You'll learn from it."

"I guess so," I say, not really wanting to learn anything else new about myself for a long time. I can still feel John's hand in mine. "I feel bad for leaving John without saying anything."

"Listen, if you think today was weird, you'll have a whole different perspective when you meet my whole family. We're world class weird," Daisy says with a chuckle. "John will be okay. I'm sure we'll see him again soon. You can't go anywhere in this town without running into the same person three times. Try to have a good night, alright?"

"Alright," I say. "I'll try. Thank you, Daisy. You have a good night, too."

"Bye!" she says, waving on her way back to the Suburban, and I watch her climb in and drive off down the long road away from Tío's.

Inside, Tío's eating instant ramen with lemon and Cholula hot sauce in the quiet of the kitchen.

"Did you have a good time?" he asks, twirling the ramen with his fork.

"It was interesting," I say, avoiding his eyes and hiding my hands behind my back. Hands, not paws or claws, but I still feel like the evidence is all over them.

"You came home early. I was expecting you later. Did something happen?"

"Honestly, yes, but you have to promise not to get mad," I say, biting my tongue through the nerves.

"I can't promise anything. Please tell me you didn't bring more attention to yourself," he says, with concerned wrinkles wriggling across his forehead.

"Well, my fingernails turned into claws," I wince. "And my hands got buff and hairy."

"In public?!" he probes, looking like he's about to have a patatus, or what one would call, a conniption fit.

"Not so public," I say. "We were in a dark movie theater. No one saw."

"Thank God!" Tío exhales, rubbing his temples with his free hand.

I slink down into the wooden chair across from him.

"Well, it's less than a week before the Full Moon," he says. "You should probably stay on the farm until it's over. Just in case," he says, switching to tapping his forehead with his knuckle.

"Yes," I say, feeling no more fight left in me for the night, and head to my room. Inside, I notice I must've left the window open. And there's a smooth rock sitting on the window-sill with a piece of paper left under it.

Call me -John, it says, with his number written under it.

My heart races, and I want to feel excited. But, I can't figure out how he knew where I live. I want to sleep, but I also never had a boy waiting for my call, so I figure I better get it out of the way instead of thinking about it all night.

"Hello?" I hear John's voice through the phone, almost as soon as I hit 'call.'

"Umm...," I struggle, not knowing what to say.

"Selena?" he asks, and I relax.

"Yeah," I finally let out.

"I guess you got my note," he says, his voice as warm and comforting as opening up a sweet, fresh tamale.

"How did you know where I live?" I ask, pacing the room with some music playing on my laptop to, hopefully, offer us some privacy from Tío's ears.

"I did a little research. Listen, I'm having a pool party tomorrow. Wanna come?"

"I would, but I don't have a swimsuit," I say, completely not expecting to need it before my mom gets to town.

"You can wear a t-shirt, and I'll lend you some shorts. Come on, it'll be fun."

"Sure, I guess," I say. "But you're gonna have to pick me up. I'm sort of grounded."

"Why are you grounded? Is that why you straight up ditched me in the movies?"

"Kinda," I say. "I'm not allowed to talk to boys, and my uncle found out we hung out."

"Oh, I see. Overprotective uncles are the best, am I right?" he laughs.

"They sure are a handful," I say, hoping Tío's seventies Rock music is keeping him isolated.

"Well, have no fear. I'll come pick you up after I get the house ready," he says, in a happy-to-accommodate way that makes me feel... nice.

"I'll be here, inside my window," I say, feeling more like a beautiful princess than the beast I felt like earlier.

7

RISKY ESCAPADES

The next morning, I wake up from a mid-morning nap to my back throbbing with a searing level of pain. Between the work on the farm and my new were-girl muscles, my body's letting me know there's no going back to being a little girl.

In the next moment, a pebble clinks against my window, and I open the curtain to find John. His dusty blonde hair and honey brown eyes shine in the sun the way he leans against his cherry red pickup truck.

I brace myself, and hoist myself out the window. If my timing is right, Tío's still somewhere in the fields, but I don't want him to hear my door or the door of the house opening or closing. I nod as casually as I can to the truck, feeling nervous in my jean shorts and faded rock band t-shirt as my body wakes up.

"Hey, let's go," I whisper, inside the truck, trying not to seem awkward.

"It's nice to see you again, too," John says, smiling at me, and grabbing my hand after shifting the truck into drive.

"Let's leave quickly, before my uncle notices I'm gone, please," I whisper, slipping my hand out of his while it's still skin and not fur.

"Alright," he says, grabbing the wheel with both hands and flooring it as much as the dirt road could handle it.

"What's that smell, though?" I ask, taking in lungfuls of artificial scented something. "It smells like… cat pee?"

"No way, not cat pee," John says, laughing. "It's my air freshener. Tropical Breeze. Is it too strong?"

"Way too strong," I say, wiping my nose from the sour burn. "I guess I don't do well with them."

"Oh, I'm sorry," he says, tossing the hanging tree from his rearview mirror into the bed of the truck as we tumble out of the yard.

"That's so much better," I say, breathing easy as the scent conditions out of the air and Fleetwood Mac takes over the conversation.

After a few songs, he pulls into a driveway off a farm road, and we approach an enormous, stone-facade mansion. Half a dozen luxury cars and SUVs sit parked in the roundabout of the driveway, and I can't help but feel a little out of place.

Inside proves just as vast and impressive as outside promised. John shows me to the kitchen first, but everyone else is already out back.

"Would you like something to drink?"

"Oh, I... don't drink alcohol," I say.

John laughs again, like guys would do when flirting with girls in school.

"I was *not* offering you alcohol. You're like, what, sixteen?"

"I'm fifteen, actually," I say, feeling embarrassed for the first time around him. Realizing I haven't told him much about me at all.

"Oh, so you're telling me I'm robbing the cradle, then?" he laughs again, this time more lightly.

"I'll take some lemonade or water," I say, recovering from the alcohol slip up, and letting us move on to something else.

"Coming right up," he says, like a gentleman, and I make my way over to the back door window to take a few long breaths.

He seems a lot more confident at home than at the mall, and I need to feel confident, too. I try to straighten my slouch and breathe. There aren't *many* people here, so it shouldn't be too bad. Just a handful of guys and girls around the really nice, crystal clear, inground pool. Laughing, volley balling, and lounging in pool recliners.

"Mystery Girl!" some yells behind me, and, yup, it's the clerk from the grocery store.

"You can call me Selena," I say. "Caleb. I remember names."

"Very impressive," he says, holding a cold soda and tiptoeing in his dripping wet bathing suit. "How did *you* manage to snag an invite to this *exclusive* party? You're so new in town, I'm surprised anyone knows you at all."

"John invited me," I say, and his smile evaporates.

"You need to be careful," Caleb whispers, making sure John can't hear him from the other side of the kitchen. "He has a reputation."

"What kind of reputation?" I whisper back, thinking John might need to be more careful of me, with my claws and all, but John's on his way over with my lemonade before Caleb can say more.

"You'll have a lot of fun with this group," Caleb says, heading out onto the patio. "Come out and meet everyone when you're ready."

"It's nice you met Caleb, he's great," John says, handing me my lemonade and a pair of swim shorts he had waiting on the counter.

"If you want, you can change in the bathroom," he suggests, making his way out back, too.

"Okay, thanks," I say hoping the howling-wolf pattern all over the shorts won't give away my secret.

Outside, Caleb and John are already splashing each other in the pool, and I can't help but notice more guys than girls at this party. I wonder if it's because of the girls who are missing. Everyone's probably afraid to let their kids out.

It's not long before the heat and sun start beading my skin with sweat, and I cannonball into the cool blue water to soothe my sizzling skin.

But as the hours pass, the energy drains from me like a hot battery. One of the other girls offers me a lounge chair to lie down and rest, but it's the heat that's getting to me. John, Caleb, and I were having a blast, and were actually good during pool volleyball against a team of two other boys and a girl.

When I got out, though, John did too. He's been right next to me since I joined the party. The water drips from his chiseled tan body like in a cologne commercial as he stands over me, laughing and talking with Caleb, who's chasing the other girls around the pool.

Little does John know, but his... perfect body and powerful presence might be to blame for the panic in my chest. He's a high school senior. The whole day feels unreal. And it'd all be ruined if I spontaneously grow claws or faint from the struggle of resisting the transformation. My stomach feels like that Christmas I ate so many tamales that I projectile vomited all over our living room and Mom had to go full nurse on me.

"Hey, you okay? Is something wrong?" John asks, as I struggle to get up to head to the bathroom, where the chilly, clean bathroom tiles were feeling like the perfect place to cool down.

"Yeah, no. I'm okay," I say, struggling to walk without swaying, which is not according to plan.

"You don't look too good," he says. "Maybe you should cool down. I have some ice packs in the freezer," he says, and helps me in the house with an arm around my shoulder.

"Ice packs sound perfect," I say, feeling the chill of excited goosebumps on every part of my skin that was hot.

"I'm sorry I'm such a mess," I say through squeezed lips in the recliner sofa.

John is holding an ice pack against my forehead, while I hold two against my cheeks, and I'm sure it looks comical. But I don't care. I feel like I need it more than anything, but the sips of more ice cold lemonade is helping, too.

"I don't think you're a mess. I think you're actually quite beautiful," he says, wiping away a drip down the length of my eyebrow.

"Then, I think you have questionable taste," I say, surprised by him.

"Don't do that," he says, with false hurt.

"Don't do what?" I say, feeling the burn of my forehead melt the ice pack, as I started to lose myself to the banging of my quickened pulse.

"Don't talk down on yourself like that," he says, almost whispering, and I realize how close his lips are to mine.

"What are you doing?" I say, moving back.

"Wait, hold still," he says, just as his lips reach mine.

And my arms forget all about the ice packs, and wind up around his neck. 'No claws,' I think with a smile. Then I lean in more, and he leans in more, too. Then the doorbell rings, and I hear familiar footsteps shuffling outside the front door.

"Shit," I say, pulling away and hearing that suction sound that kissers make, for the first time coming from my mouth!

"What?" John says, looking confused.

"He found me," I say. And sure enough, when John opens the front door, Tío Julio's standing with his trusty shotgun at his hip, immediately finding me behind John.

"Selena Lucia Sol-Valencia, come here, now!" he demands.

"Sí Tío," I say, back under his jurisdiction, whether I like it or not. I'm guilty. I went against our agreement. I left without saying anything. I know what's coming next.

"Sorry, John," I say, his eyes now bulging out of their sockets, and looking like he could probably use an ice pack. My first and last kiss, all in less than five minutes.

"Get in the car," Tío Julio says, straining with anger.

"It was my idea, all this," I say, hoping he'll leave John alone. It's a blessing everyone else is still in the back to not see this.

"I'm sorry, Julio," John says, before turning to me. "I'm sorry, Selena."

"I don't ever want to find her brought here again, and I never want to see your cherry-red pickup on my land. You got that?" Tío says, and I cringe. Tío's way of speaking makes words cut deep, and it's clear John isn't immune.

"I just..." I say, trying to say something to make things better as Tío yanks his way back into his truck. But he won't look at me.

"¡Ni una palabra!" he says, reversing us back out of the long, wooded driveway. The silence, thicker than Gel-Suavecíto, sin suave.

"When I was nine years old, I was attacked, Selena. I was visiting family in Mexico, looking up at the stars off in a field by the house. I saw a shadowed figure jump out at me, and I don't remember much after that," Tío says, finally parking in front of our house.

When I don't speak, he shakes his head, looking for the words to continue. I never know what to say when adults speak from places so deep inside that it makes them cry.

"It took me years to recover, and most of the time I was all alone. Here, on the farm. Our whole family moved from Mexico after that. They'd suffered for decades, as you might know. But here, at least we don't have to live with all the curses of our past. At least here we can focus on the curses of the present. And presently, your dad came by last night."

"What?!" I say, not believing him, but he looks serious.

"Good, now that I know I have your attention. When you leave the house without a note telling me where you are or who you're with, I'm rightfully going to get upset," he says, wagging his finger in my face.

"Okay," I say, wanting to get past this and on to the parts about my dad, even if Tío's story was interesting, too.

"Second, you were told explicitly not to leave the house because we don't know how you're going to react around young men," he says.

"Well, we didn't explicitly discuss the young men part," I say, wanting to know more about that, too.

"And third, mija, I was scared! Girls are disappearing left and right, and I don't know how it's happening. Do you understand how dangerous it is if I can't even detect it? How would I explain myself to your mother, my only sister, if something bad happens to you. I couldn't live with myself. Can you see? Can you understand?" he says, eyes watering.

"Oh, I understand Tío, but what I don't understand is how you found me."

"That boy's awful air freshener...," he says with a grimace. "...and the smell of your soap, the lavender. It's very distinctive."

"Oh, well that makes sense, but did you really need to bring a shotgun?" I say, needing to burn through the mortifying questions in my head before getting back to *Dad*.

"I didn't know who took my sobrina. How could I not come prepared? Any more questions, before you're on toilet duty?" he says, raising a quizzical brow.

"I have a few more, actually," I say, hoping I won't lose track.

"Great," Tío says, sitting back in his seat.

"Why was I *dying* in the sun? Even being in the pool drained me."

"Ah, yes. Rule number five: Dress modestly. I made that rule because if your skin is exposed to the sun for too long, the energy you have drains out of you. It's the moon that increases our powers. Solar depletes us. That's why we work so early in the morning, before it's sunny out. But our energy increases to its maximum capacity on the Full Moon. And, for the better, that's the only night the power grows uncontrollable. Except if there's a Blue Moon. Then it's even stronger. Then, the moon is at its maximum fullness. Which we're also coming up on."

"I can't believe I have to live by all these stupid rules. It's so frustrating! Why can't I just be a normal teenager?" I say, holding my head in my hands. "Where's my dad, now?"

"He'll be back in the morning. He wanted to talk to me before just surprising you. He asked Santos where you were, and didn't want to miss your first Full Moon. This doesn't mean you're off the hook for today, though."

"Wait, my first WHAT?"

THE DANCE OF THE DUELING WEREWOLVES

The next morning I wake up sore and hungry from all the cleaning Tío had me do for running away. The smell of frying eggs came to me even in my sleep, now. Making my drooling situation a little out of hand. In the kitchen, a man who isn't my tío is cooking at the stove, and the table is already set with glasses of orange juice and all.

"Have a seat, mi princesa, mi chula, mi reina," the strange man says, and a few seconds later he's loading my plate with eggs, tortilla, salsa, and refried beans. Then kisses my forehead. I remember my father was the only one who ever called me his beautiful princess queen, based on what my tío Santos would tell me about him. Could this stranger in front of me actually be my dad?

Before I can decide on what to say, Tío Julio comes in from feeding the chickens, and I look between the two of them as they exchange glances.

"¿Esos huevos rancheros?" I ask, wanting to focus on the food without ruining another meal.

"It is a gift of a delicacy," Dad smirks, nodding at Tío. "And well within the bounds of your tío's rules."

"Thanks," I smile, unleashing on the meal.

"It is good to see you, mija," Dad says, his eyes watering the way Tío's did last night. It's crazy how just growing up can make the strongest adults cry.

"It's good to see you, too," I say, not exactly sure how to feel.

I never had a proper father-daughter relationship. He left when I was three, but now, with him in the room with me, I'm not sure how to act.

"So, I hear our little girl is a woman now," Dad says, sitting down across from me.

"What?" I say, almost spitting out my food.

"Your quinceañera," he says, looking more confused than I do.

"Oh, right," I say, glad he isn't talking about anything else.

"You know, if you haven't transformed yet, that means we can go out hunting together for the first time, as a family," he says.

"I don't know if that's a good idea," Tío answers back. "We don't know how she's going to react under the Full Moon; it's a Blue Moon. You know that's extra potent."

"No le haces caso mija, you're not scared are you? We can handle anything, together. You'll see how much fun it is to let loose and howl at the moon with your old man," he says, patting my hand across the table.

"But, I did turn," I say. "At my quinceañera, right Tío?"

"You more, half-turned, from what your mom explained," Tío says.

"Oh, then the Blue Moon will definitely bring it out of you!" Dad says, chomping on a bite of his huevos rancheros the way I eat mine. Full on messy.

"Ay Dios, dame paciencia!" Tío mutters under his breath.

"What, you don't trust me, Tío?" I ask, wanting to keep the two men talking while I figure out my own messy thoughts as everything becomes almost too much.

"No, I don't. For a number of reasons. One, you're a teenage girl, which automatically classifies you as a 'hot mess.' On top of that, you have no self-control. I haven't even gotten the chance to *start* your training with everything going on the last few days, and werewolves have killed their best friends, have killed people they loved the most, have harmed everyone close to them. They don't respect age or gender or relationship. I actually know of a werewolf who attacked his own baby daughter when he was in the depths of his lycan."

"Oh, geez, I'd never do that," I say, shuddering at the thought.

"You say that now, but when you're lycan, your frontal cortex isn't working. Not that your fifteen year old frontal cortex is much to work with," he says, flicking my forehead. "As lycan's, we rely on the cerebellum, the pituitary, and the hypothalamus."

"How do you even know all this?" I ask.

"He's a smart man," Dad says, sitting for the lesson with more respect than I expected.

"I may just be a farmer, but I do read, you know. People used to read books before they had all this electronic stuff," Tío says, looking flustered. "Plus, I have a bunch of medical textbooks from when your mom was in nursing school. She gave them to me after she graduated."

"So, what do you do when you're a lycan?" I ask, looking between the two men.

"I do what I've been disciplined to do: Restrain myself in a cage down in the basement," Tío says, without blinking.

"Oh, that sounds... horrifying!" I say, picturing Tío in the cage I pictured Daisy's mom in when she told me about her mom locking herself in the basement on the Full Moon.

"I do what I must do to keep everyone safe," Tío says, looking down at his feet.

"Is that why you moved away? So, you wouldn't hurt us?" I ask, finally connecting the dots. As a Sol, he needs to be alone. He needs solitude and peace.

"It's a reason, but it is not the only reason. Most of the time, a Sol needs to fly solo," he says.

"How do you cope with everything, Dad?" I ask, looking to my father for an answer for the first time.

"For a Valencia, life is tough, too," Dad starts, resting his elbows on the table and getting serious. "As the alpha of the pack, it's even more difficult. And it's even more difficult having a child who's half Sol. For instance, I'm not allowed to cross the border except for right now, with the permissions from the other elders of our pack. And not because of their own feelings, but because the head of the Valencia pack is so tied to our ancestral land, that my absence could be enough to destroy the progress we've made in balancing the land and bay with the moon and tides. Our people are prospering, even if I, and we, are sacrificing. You and your mother have been the greatest blessings of my life, but your mother, being a Sol, is tied to these lands you've inhabited your whole life. You can thrive in either place, I believe, but your mom cannot. I cannot. Our people cannot. You're different though, and that's why it's so important for me to be here for your first Full Moon. And for your first transformation!"

"No," Tío Julio says. "That's why it's important she learns how to discipline the lobo inside, before she goes loco!"

The two are now talking more to each other than to me, and in the mess of thoughts and emotions and tempers, the walls start closing in on me. I can't pick a side. I don't know myself any more than I did before my quinceañera, and I start to regret that I asked my questions in the first place. My lungs constrict the way Mom squeezes límones, but I'm afraid I have no more juice for the menudo.

"I need some air," I say, staggering to my feet, and heading for the back door.

Un ataque de pánico is what Mexicans call a panic attack. My heart races. My palms drip with sweat. My head spins, and only sitting in the shade against the house, in the breeze of chicken clucks, can I slow my breathing. I find myself hugging my knees in the soft dirt, whimpering like a scared dog under a thunderstorm.

"Selena, estás bien? Are you okay?" Tío asks, against the smack of the back door.

"I just freaked out, okay. This is all a bit much for me, and seeing my dad is just... a little... overstimulating. I can only take so much change at once!"

"It is alright, mija, let it out," Tío Julio says, rubbing my neck. "I know, it's not easy seeing your dad after so long, but I promise you, I won't go anywhere. I'll always be here for you. And we're going to make this all easier for you. Let us be the ones to worry. Come here."

Tío opens his arms around me, and for the first time since I was a kid, we hug. And for the first time since I arrived, I feel like we're real allies instead of adversaries.

"Your dad is giving you some space, but we'll plan for him to take you to dinner before the Full Moon, if you're up for it. You two deserve some time together after so long. *Now* is always the best time to smooth over old wounds. But doing it right, and on your terms is always the best way forward. Te amo, mi sobrina."

"Y te amo a ti, Tío. And, thank you. For everything."

"Ay, Selena. I'll miss you when you finally leave, if your mom decides to move away again. I think I spend too much time alone with my thoughts."

"Well, maybe you should get a dog or something," I say, remembering the fluffy white dog I saw herding the sheep.

"You know, that's not the world's worst idea. Maybe we should go to the shelter and see if the right dog is out there. Why don't you take a rest, I'll finish the farm work, and then we can head to the county shelter?"

"That sounds good to me," I say, thanking God for the chance to do something stress free for the first time since... hanging out with Sophia.

"Hola, my name is Consuelo. I'm in charge of fostering and adoptions here. How are you today?" A cheery brunette in bright orange scrubs waves over to us from her desk as soon as we walk into the dated and crumbling interior of the county shelter.

"We're doing alright," Tío says. "We're interested in adopting a dog today," he adds, as I'm pulled toward the glass doors of the "Kitty Koral," by the fluffy kitties wobbling around their drowsy mothers. Behind them, the room is lined with cages full of cats of every color and size. And despite my being excited at the sight of them, they all hiss at me, even from afar.

"No cats," Tío says, pulling me by the arm. "We're here for a dog, remember?"

"Wow," Consuelo says. "I'm pretty sure the cats don't want to go home with you, girl."

"The feeling's mutual, I guess," I say, following them away from the panicked cats, and feeling disturbed by their reaction to me.

Consuelo leads us to the kennel, and once inside, starts introducing us to the first dog.

"This is Luna. She's been here the longest," Consuelo says, with a concerned tremble slipping into her voice. Luna's a medium size black rottweiler, cowering in the back corner of the kennel.

"She's such a sweet girl but... she doesn't always warm up to people well."

"I see," Tío says, stepping closer to take a better look, but the dog growls, and he backs off. I step closer. She's a little apprehensive, but she starts to approach the bars. And eventually, sniffs my hand and allows me to pet her.

For some reason beyond my control, I rub my forehead with hers, and she rubs mine back. And somehow, we both know she's coming home with us. When I lean back, she looks up at me and at Tío, with her gentle hazel eyes, begging us to take her home.

Consuelo babbles on about Luna's shots, diet, and routines, but I nod along not listening to any of it.

"But she doesn't really take to men."

That catches my attention.

"It'll take a bit of building trust, but then she's great. Her intake card says she can herd animals, so really she's not just looking for a home, she's also looking for a job," Consuelo adds with a grin.

"Well, my sister and Selena will be around to help me with her until she warms up to me," Tío says. "But is Luna the one, Selena? What do you think?"

"She's so sweet!" I say, already decided.

"She sure is," he says, looking down at us. "It could be good to have a guard dog or a herd dog for the farm. I guess she sounds perfect."

"Great! I'll bring over the paperwork! And you can take her out on a leash. We have some extras if you didn't bring one."

Consuelo hurries back down the cage lined hall while the dogs stalk Tío Julio and I, and sniff the air, but for some reason don't dare to bark.

"Now remember, there's usually a three day decompression period, followed by three weeks of settling in. And then there's the three month bond building timeframe. Sometimes it takes longer," says Consuelo, returning with the paperwork and leash.

"Sounds great," I say. "By the time Mom comes, we'll all be best buds!"

"Lucky us," Tío says, laughing at my delight. "Now let's get out of here before you fall in love with another dog. One is plenty."

Then Tío signs on the dotted line, and Luna is ours.

Outside, we struggle to get Luna into the cab of the truck. She's not bad, she's just playfully excited to be with me.

"Maybe we should just let her sit on your lap," Tío says, looking down at Luna wagging her tail.

"I'd be okay with that!" I say, excited by the thought. "Will your nerves be okay?"

"They'll be okay. Luna doesn't make me as nervous as humans do," he explains, holding open the truck door as I climb in with Luna.

"Why did the dogs sniff at you but not bark or growl?" I ask, rolling down the window as he shuts us in.

"It could be because I'm a man-werewolf," he says, in the frame of the window. "Sometimes it has its perks being an alpha."

"So, why did Luna growl at you?"

"She's an interesting dog. She's probably as temperamental as I am, hearing how she doesn't warm up to people much."

"Then is it weird that Luna warmed up to me so fast?"

"Well, you're not an alpha, and you're not quite only human. But you haven't fully transformed yet, either. She might just be confused about you and not know how to feel yet."

"Oh, thanks," I say. "I was expecting a, 'she loves you just that much,' or something."

"Well, you already know that the lycan and animal worlds are more complicated than that, Selena. But Luna, with a name like that, will show us a lot more about who we are than who she really is. In a way only la Luna can."

9

TEA AND TRANSFORMATION

Despite having the fan on high, I wake up sweltering and sticking to my sheets. I toss and turn, but my skin is ablaze, and my hair follicles are stiff and sensitive again. Luna wakes, too, and whimpers at the sight of me from across the room.

"Tío!" I cry, unable to bite back the pain.

"What's the matter?!" Tío asks, bursting through the door. Luna barks a strong bark, but then whimpers after recognizing Tío.

"Everything hurts!" I cry. "My skin's on fire, my head's numb, and I don't know what's wrong with me!"

I check for paws, a tail, a snout, but nothing's out of the ordinary.

"Those are all signs of transformation, but the Full Moon isn't out for three more days," Tío says, looking unsure of himself.

"Wait!" I cry, as a hot wet flood surges down my legs. I lift my sheet, and see the spread of scarlet blood peel from my pajama pants.

"Mija, that's your period! This really is going to be your first moon!"

"No, no, no, no, no! I really didn't think it was ever going to come," I say, genuinely amazed and disappointed at the same time. Being a woman is great, but not having to deal with *this* and being a woman, would make life a little easier.

"Now that we know, I should tell you something. But you might want to get cleaned up first. I have a lesson and a story to tell you."

"Fine," I say, annoyed by the mess, but eager to be clean. Whatever lesson Tío has to tell me can wait. "I have a whole womanhood's worth of time to fill, now."

"I'll make you some jasmine tea. It has properties that will slow down your transformation."

"That would've been useful earlier," I say, staring up at the ceiling.

"Better late than never!" Tío calls back through the door.

Slowly, I get up and make my way to the bathroom. The tile's cool against my forehead while I wait for the shower to kick into gear and start streaming instead of dripping. My bones ache under the cool water, and I cry into the cascading flow.

I try to focus on my racing heart and try to steady my breath the way I was taught. But, somehow, through the darkness of my closed eyes I see a girl, bound by the wrists and ankles with a blindfold covering her eyes. Terrified. Struggling against the ropes sawing into her soft flesh...

"Who are you? What's happening to you?" I wonder out loud, then hear Tío's footsteps and a firm knock on the bathroom door.

"Are you okay in there?" he asks, voice on edge.

"I'm fine," I say, not sure of what to think, but hopeful that Daisy might have some insights.

In my room I find a steaming mug of jasmine tea on the nightstand, and the aroma of it plays me like a symphony harp. I go from feeling like I just left a lockroom shower to feeling like I entered a spa, and it... relaxes me. The specs of tea vapor fill the air like the steam of a sauna, and I sip cautiously, realizing my vision is better... like, a lot better.

I want to call Daisy and ask her about my eyes and the girl I saw, but my body feels drained. I lie back on the bed, still wrapped in towels, and drink my jasmine tea. After I finish, I fall helplessly, and thankfully, into a well of deep, profound sleep. I dream as the pregnant moon wheels itself from one side of the starry night sky to the other, bringing us one day closer to the Blue Moon.

The next morning, I butter my toast while Tío Julio makes me more jasmine tea in a pot on the stove. I dreamed all night of the girl bound by her wrists, but my body, at least, didn't have any more surprising discharges or transformations while I slept. And the discomfort of my period is, surprisingly, more quelled by Tío's brew.

Daisy and John had both called and texted, but I wasn't ready to respond earlier. Luna needed taking out as soon as I awoke, and I want to get an answer for Daisy before I call her back with my questions. Her question, though, is an invitation for me and Tío to a church picnic, and

I'm not hopeful in his answer being a yes. Not after everything we've already been through together, but it's worth a shot.

"How are you feeling?" Tío asks from the stove.

"I'm better than yesterday. That tea really helps."

"Yes, it's the best for most things. Have a seat. You know, during the Full Moon all female lycans transform and have their periods. But the Blue Moon is special. Female lycans transform and go into heat, so it's the only time they're fertile. Now, offspring conceived during a Full Moon would be born a werewolf. They're called 'Naturals' and don't need to be bitten or scratched to have the lycan curse. Naturals tend to have a much easier time during their first transformations. With the Blue Moon and your first transformation coming, your body will react in ways I can't predict. Fertile or not, your body isn't equipped to bear lycan offspring. But it could very well attract males to the area."

"Thankfully, the Blue Moon's still three days away," I say, looking for a bright side.

"That's right," Tío says. "Your cycles will eventually align with every other female lycan over time, but males will sense you... probably starting with yesterday."

"Great," I say, still determined to live my life and enjoy the few days of semi-normal life I still have left.

"It's like you're living in a novella, still on Episodio Uno, de La Vida Selena Sol-Valencia."

"Well, let me ask you something now," I say, wanting to think about anything but myself. "Why don't you go to church?" I ask, as Tío sets down a fresh steaming cup of tea and takes a seat to eat with me.

"What? Are you serious? Eat your food," he says, waving me off.

"Church, why?" I ask, pushing it. I won't push too far, but family drama is worth two no's.

"Where's this coming from?" he asks, eyeing me suspiciously.

"I've just been wondering. Plus, Daisy and her mom invited us to their church's picnic tomorrow. It might be good to bring Luna around and show her off. In case she gets loose one day, everyone will know she's ours."

"Yeah," Tío says. "Well, I was going to tell you this story anyway, so I guess now's the best time. You'll get your answer at the end, I promise."

"Okay," I say, settling into my seat.

"Now, I know your change of life is a little different, but back when I was your age, it wasn't acceptable to be gay," Tío says, taking a sip of his tea. "So, when I was having those thoughts and feelings... You know... That you're having... The teenage hormones... Well, let's just say it made me feel like I was an outsider."

"But Tío, aren't things different now?" I ask, thinking about how open people are in the cities.

"Well, gay maybe, but certainly not werewolf. We'll never be accepted by regular people. You're gonna need to learn that for your own safety."

"What about giving people a chance?" I say, realizing how much I sound like my mom, but still feeling right.

"Mija, I already did that, and it got me nowhere, except hurt and betrayed," he says, eyes growing full with tears. "Let me set the scene for you, mija. Forty years ago... When I was about your age now, I stood outside a small church in Fullerton. The sun was shining on a bunch of guys playing flag football. Being new to town, I introduced myself to them on one of their breaks, and they invited me to a costume party there later that night. The theme was, dress as your favorite celebrity."

"That's promising," I say, adding my own bit of hope into the story I know has to have a tragic turn.

"Well, you'll see. I was excited. It was my first party in town, and costume parties were always my favorite growing up. So, I went all out. I put on a long black wig, a rhinestone bedazzled dress, sky-high heels. I wanted to be the star of the show, and I wanted to win best costume. As soon as I got to the church, I noticed the boy Trevor that I talked with on the field. He was decked out as James Bond in a baby blue '70s jumpsuit and black sunglasses. And he noticed me too, and even recognized me."

"'Dude, are you dressed as Cher? She's a girl!' he shouted, and burst out laughing."

"'She's my favorite celebrity...' I said, on the verge of tears as everyone around us started looking, pointing, and laughing at me."

"'Are you like, gay or something,' he said, and with everyone staring and mocking, I was mortified."

"I said I had to go, and ran away on my two pencil thin high heels. Clacking through the church, across the parking lot, and into the darkness. Until nobody could see my mascara streaking down my face in thick black trails. Society may be different in the cities, but I've found inside churches, at least in these rural areas, to be the incubators of hate and discrimination. For the were and queer alike."

"Wow," I say, feeling really bad.

My worst moments were at my quinceañera and at John's house, and neither came close to Tío's Cher nightmare. "That guy Trevor's an asshole! It was a costume party! Dress however you like!"

"Ay, mi sobrina. If it wasn't Trevor who said something, somebody else there would have, and it all would have ended the same way. In this country, and historically, if you don't live in a place where you're supported, then you must flee or suffer the circumstances as they are. And that means keeping to yourself around the immature and ignorant. If I had a friend like you back in the day, maybe things could have been different. I was fabulous! But, I was insecure. I was afraid. I've been holding a grudge against the church ever since. I mean, I still pray, but no other people are part of my faith."

He sips delicately at his Earl Grey, looking like a man who's lived with pain.

"Well, I'm here now, and it'd be a shame to let insecure kids from almost thirty years ago dictate what you do now as an adult. You're different. Heck, maybe they're different too. I'll tell Daisy we're good for the picnic. I can't wait to show her to Luna!"

"Ay, Selena. I'll compromise with you on this one for now, but I'll be the one needing the support dog, if I can even make it there without freaking out first."

10

PICNICS AND PREJUDICE

"This is not a good idea," Tío Julio says, pulling into the church parking lot the next day.

"Come on, don't be such a chicken. It's just a church picnic!" I say, petting Luna, who's propped up on the window with her paws, looking out the glass at the small group of people scattered around the church grounds. I hunt for Daisy and her mom, but only find their white Suburban dazzling like a pearl in the collection of rundown pickup trucks.

"They might not welcome us, you know. God, I'm so nervous. I haven't gone to a public function in like... ten years!" Tío Julio says, fiddling with his bolo after we park.

"Daisy said more of our neighbors will be here. It'll be perfect! Maybe you could even see if Shirley has a gay brother or cousin. You never know! She seemed to like you. And if it gets weird, we'll just pick up our deviled eggs and leave," I say, looking at him with sympathy.

"You think Shirley might know someone gay?" he asks, looking interested for the first time all day.

"She might! I'll ask Amelia, too. We can find you *somebody*."

"Okay," Tío says, opening his door. "If you say so."

"'Crossroads Christian Church' sounds pretty progressive to me," I say, with a little false courage as Tío and I make our way across the parking lot. Tío laughs, thankfully. The more I make him smile, the less I think about my own problems.

"I'll believe it when I see it," he says, smiling back at me.

"Hey there, neighbor!" Shirley says, appearing in, and waving us into the church doors. I expected to see her sheep herding dog with her, but she's leashless. Luna, leashed and padding her way at my feet, seems happy to see Shirley too, but Tío looks to be struggling.

"Hello, Shirley," Tío says, attempting a smile under the brim of his bolo.

"It's so good to see you, Julio. And Selena! It's good to see you're getting along in town. And who's this new pup?"

"Hi Shirley," I say, feeling more like I made the right decision in pushing Tío to come. "This is Luna. She's our new farm dog."

"And what a precious pup she is! You'll have to come inside and say hi. I think Daisy's somewhere in the back. The boys, or men, are out back by the grill. Julio, can I show you around the place? I'll introduce you to whoever you don't know, but I've got someone special I've been meaning to introduce you to."

"That sounds great!" I say, nudging Tío in the side at the suggestion. "I told you!" I whisper, and Tío clears his throat from nervousness.

"That'd be great," Tío says, and I'm more proud of him than ever. I could almost cry.

"I'll go find Daisy. Do you want Luna?" I ask Tío, holding out the leash. He looks down at Luna and back at me, and then to Shirley.

"You take her to meet Daisy. I'll be busy with the adults," Tío says, and follows a delighted Shirley into the church and down a hall.

"So she was bound at the wrists?" Daisy asks, thinking harder than I ever want to try.

"Yeah, with rope. I don't know what it means. Do were-girls usually get visions like that?" I ask, wondering if I should have maybe asked Tío before exposing my unusual hallucinations, or... abilities.

"They could, I guess. It's more of a witchy talent than a lycan talent. I'll have to ask my mom more about it. I wish she had prepared me for these things better, instead of trying to keep me in the dark to find out on my own. All these girls are missing, you're having visions of a bound girl, and hmmm... I got nothing. Luna is *so* cute though! When did you get her? Why didn't you tell me?"

"Well, that's the other thing I have to tell you. I'm officially not a late bloomer anymore, and I had a panic attack at John's house a couple days ago."

"For a new girl, you sure know how to make friends and fill your days!" Daisy says. "So, you *are* turning tomorrow, though! A first transformation on a Blue Moon sounds like a special thing. We'll have to look into that, too. I'll do some research. As for John, are you two like a *thing* now?"

"Honestly, no," I say. "I thought it could be cool to maybe go on a couple dates, but I can't trust myself around *anybody*, let alone a teenage boy with hormones as raging as my own. Tío said I could go *into heat* on the Blue Moon."

"Oh yeah," Daisy says. "If you go into heat, you might black out and go feral. It happens to teenage lycan who haven't learned to control their inner lobos. You could wake up a whole day later and not remember a thing. That's what I've been settling on, though. I think the disappearances are linked to a feral, new, uncontrollable teenage werewolf. It's one of the only things that makes sense, given the sporadic nature of the disappearances."

"Interesting," I say. "We'll have to stay vigilant. I've also only answered John back a couple of times because I don't know what I should do about him, either. Everything about this is getting in the way of my life."

"Well, I found you because of your were-girlness, and we're now friends! That's one good thing!"

"You're right," I say, petting Luna, and feeling love for her, too.

"And you better figure out what to say, because John's here. He's out back by the grill. We could go talk with him."

"Oh, great," I say, rolling my eyes. The church property is pretty scarce except for mowed law and sparse tall old trees that give a lot of shade out back, but the front is still hot, baking with the parking lot in the sun. "I don't know if it's a good idea. Last time I saw him, Tío was pointing a gun at him, and I'm kind of responsible for it. I had John secretly pick me up."

"Well, you'll either have to smooth that over, or burn that bridge quickly, because here he comes," Daisy says, looking the other way. And sure enough, I hear John's footsteps coming around the front of the church to where Daisy and I are sitting on the front steps in the shade with Luna at our feet. There's no time to run and no time to hide.

"Hey, Daisy, Selena," John says. "It's good to see you two. I didn't know you were gonna be here."

"My mom organizes these events," Daisy says. "Like, *every* one you've ever been to."

"Oh, right," John says, rubbing his forehead in the sun. "I forgot about that."

"Well, come have a seat. It's nice to see you again," I say, gesturing to the space beside me as my nerves start to kick in. But Luna rubs the fur of her face against my hand, and I remember there's really nothing that can hurt me. Tío's inside, with his voice filtering through the open windows. And Daisy is more of a guard dog than any real dog I could find. And I have a feeling Amelia could rip somebody's head clean off if she was inclined to do so.

But as John steps into the shade of the church-house shadow, Luna starts to growl. A few more steps, and Luna's bearing her teeth and barking!

"I'm sorry, I forgot!" I say, holding Luna tight, to try to calm her down. "Luna's sensitive around men. She's only just gotten used to Tío."

"Oh," John says, looking more uncomfortable than he did before. "I'm not always good around dogs, either. They make me kind of nervous."

"How ironic," Daisy says, laughing to herself and giving me a raised-eyed look.

"Ah, John!" I hear Tío say, coming out of the church's front doors. "I wanted to say I'm sorry for the other night. Selena and I are working on our communication. I had no idea what was going on."

"Hey, I hear you," John says. "No harm, no foul. I would have been nervous, too. I'll be sure to speak with you before we hang out again."

"That's very admirable for a young man," Tío says, crouching behind me and getting close to my ear. "Shirley's gay cousin is with her! He's a little younger than me, but he's flirting!"

"In God's house?" I say in faux shock, playing with him. "Get back in there and get to know him, then!"

"I will, ma. Thank you, thank you, thank you," he whispers. "Food's ready in ten minutes around back," Tío says to all of us, and heads back inside.

Around back, John is still nervous around Luna, and Luna is still nervous around John. But Daisy and I are having a great time watching the two of them and laughing at their flinches from one another.

"Man, I wish we got to finish the movie with you," I say, as John finishes recapping what we missed after we ditched him.

"Hey, we met before?" a woman asks me, walking up to Tío.

"Ah, probably not," Tío says.

"I'm Sheri, Sheri Lynn Butler," she says, smiling at Tío in a hungry kind of way. "I'm your neighbor on the East side of your farm. It's nice to meet you."

"Nice to meet you, Sheri Lynn Butler," I say, extending my hand to shake, surprising myself with the small town gesture.

"Nice to meet you too, doll," Sheri says, shaking my hand.

"And Selena, this is Eddie, Shirley's cousin. He built a tiny home in the woods on her land and works there remotely. Isn't that cool?" Tío says, raising his hand for a middle-aged white guy with the same strawberry blonde hair as Shirley. Eddie waves over, and heads in our direction after leaving the church back door.

"That is cool!" I say, fully into supporting him and everything he and Eddie could one day be. Even if I can't see to the end of the week in my own life, it doesn't mean my mind's stopped fantasizing about the futures of others.

"Hi Selena," Eddie says, fully embodying the outdoorsy fit-vibes, wearing a pair of thin shoes that separate his toes. "It's nice to meet my new neighbor!"

"Hi, Eddie, it's nice to meet you, too," I say. "I hope to see you around the farm, since you live so close. I'll introduce you to our sassy chickens, and it looks like Luna might actually like you!"

"And I love Luna," Eddie says, crouching down for Luna as she plays at his feet, sniffing his toe-shoes.

"She likes you better than she likes me, go figure," Tío says, laughing, and touching Eddie on the shoulder as we all watch Luna with amusement.

"Well now, let's settle down and eat," Shirley says, coming over to the picnic area with another bowl propped on her hand like a waitress and sets it down on the red and white checked picnic tablecloth. And everyone takes a seat where they can.

I'm between Daisy and John, with Luna laying on the grass at the end of the table beside Daisy. Tío Julio, Eddie, and Shirley sit across from us, with Amelia, Sheri Lynn, and others scattered around.

"To get introductions out of the way," Sheri Lynn says. "Julio brought his niece who's staying with him, Selena. She's starting school with Daisy and John soon, and this is their first church picnic! Let's give her a welcoming round of applause... I'll introduce everyone to you Selena. On my left is Karol with a K. Karol runs the church with Thomas sitting next to her. They're married. Then we have Susan, and across from her we have Michael. They're married and own the grocery store. They started humble, and will die humble if they have anything to say about it. Too humble, if you ask me, but the eyes of the Lord are the only mirrors they look in. Patty and John senior are out of town for the week, but young Johnny's here. And, everyone else you know. We're a small group this week, but families are traveling before the school year starts. Happens like this every year."

"Yet it couldn't be more different from any other year, with all the girls gone missing," Karol says, her pastel pink cardigan clinging to her white linen dress.

"Oh Karol, here we go again," Thomas says, his green jeans and brown boots an interesting choice against his blue checked shirt.

"I don't let my girls out at night, period," says Susan. "I even kept them home today, because you never know. At least I got the cameras, and they all have phones. As soon as girls started disappearing, I got the family plan."

"What do you think is the cause?" Tío asks, piling a plate with potato salad.

"Wolves," Sheri says without a thought, causing Daisy and I both to choke on our Hi-C punch.

"Wolves?" I ask, through the acid burn. "Wolves aren't native to California, are they? Aren't the dangerous species around here humans? Isn't it more likely they've been kidnapped?"

"Well, men are the scariest animals out there, no offense," Sheri says, waving off the looks of the men around the picnic table. "They're the main perpetrators across the country, it's a fact. They carry out like eighty or ninety percent of crimes, violent and non-violent. This is exactly why I say we need Jesus."

"Exactly," I say, adding my two cents to anything that got us off the topic of anything closely related to wolves. And fully conscious of John sitting next to me. I can almost feel my hormones releasing throughout my body, and clamouring up my mind with racing thoughts.

"But, you know," Sheri says. "I've lived in Wyoming, and I think the wolves are migrating here. Sometimes I feel like I can smell them in the air at home. Maybe 'cause my farm touches the state forest? I don't know."

"Well, I guess it's time I dust off my shotgun," Thomas says.

"Well Julio's is ready to go," John adds, and I lean into it.

"Yeah, we should join the search parties," I say to Tío, looking at him for help.

"I can bring my shotgun with me, if you think it will help," Tío says between bites of potato salad. "This is *so* good! I haven't had any in years."

"That's my special recipe," Eddie says, leaning into Tío and spooning himself some of the potato salad from the bowl.

"You do a great job," Tío says, half flirting. "I'll have to keep that in mind."

"Let me know if you ever need a reminder," Eddie says, full flirting back. "I got you."

"Thanks," Tío says, clearly living a daydream behind his smiling, squinted eyes.

"It'll help, all right. The only good wolf is a dead wolf," Michael asserts.

"Aren't they only dangerous when winter is coming? I don't know if it makes sense that it's wolves since we're so far from winter. I mean, look at all the cows around here," I say, trying to ease the tension. "They have way more meat than a few boney human girls."

"You have a point, but I'll find them," Sheri says. "One way or another. The wolves, the girls... mark my words."

After surviving our first encounter at Crossroads Christian Church, Tío decides to fit in a lesson on self control. We both did great throughout the day, but my hormones were on fire around John. And by the time we left, my shirt was wet with sweat, to the point that Daisy had to steal me away to the bathroom to blot.

"Kneel with me," Tío says, rolling out baby pink and blue yoga mats across the small living room floor.

"Yoga?" I ask, wondering if I'm dreaming.

"Rule Eight: Meditation!" he says.

"And... how do you expect me to meditate after eating all that food?" I stuffed my face a few times at the picnic, and again right before we left. Shirley even mentioned it was the only time they never had leftovers.

"Meditation will help," Tío says. "Entering into a meditative mind will help you get through panic attacks and will help you control your temper before and after you transform. And, if I'm being completely honest, it's the only reason Shirley still has a pulse after being my neighbor for twenty-five years. Even if she's really not that bad."

A wolfish grin spreads across his face, and I roll my eyes as I lower myself to my knees.

"Okay, let's do this," I say, stretching from side to side with one arm high at a time.

"Close your eyes. Hands on knees. And take a deep, cleansing breath," Tío instructs, and I follow every direction as he says it, settling into myself as my body settles into the plush of the mat.

"Should I be seeing colors? Am I doing this right?" I ask, wondering why fireworks of colors are dancing around the blackness of my closed eyes.

"Seeing colors? No, that's not normal. Wait, you're distracting me. Stop it," he says next to me. "This could save a life one day. Your life. The ability to think clearly when your mind is no longer your own is critical."

"Okay," I sigh. "Let me try again."

11

THE BLUE MOON

There are many ways to describe my father. *Life of the party.* *Glib.* *Gregarious.* *Never sure, if he's coming, or going.* I heard them all growing up. I have one picture of him from back in the '80s hidden in my journal. Mom always thought it was hidden from me in the garage. It's a photo of him in California with a head full of brown curls, a mustache, and white pants that were a bit too tight. But the heartstopper was the black mesh, sleeveless shirt.

Meanwhile, my modest mother stands like a stoic beside him in a shapeless sweater and long skirt. The woman who only wears red lipstick for special occasions. The woman who sacrifices, working eighteen and twenty hour shifts some nights. Priding herself on saving money for my new uniforms for school every year. She was much younger, then, but, even then, she clearly hated shopping for herself and keeping up with the latest fashion trends.

I, on the other hand, like looking nicely dressed. I haven't grown much taller over the years, but my hips widen consistently, which makes wardrobe shopping difficult. I fit into a woman's size ten, while my other classmates are wearing size zeroes and twos.

Dad called for me early in the day to double check that we were still on for dinner, and Tío couldn't refuse the father-daughter time. I couldn't either. Though, Tío also seemed to welcome a chance to go see Eddie for the night, and I can't blame him. I wanted my own time with Dad, and I wanted answers to some of the questions I've had forever. And we all plan on being back at Tío's before it gets dark to brave the Blue Moon together.

The authentic Mexican restaurant Dad takes me to is a few miles south of Tío's house, and it comes alive with mariachi music on the loudspeakers clipped to the ceiling next to the decorative lace-like punched paper banners fluttering on their strings in every color. But nowhere he could take me would make me feel less weird sitting across from a person who was supposed to be there my whole life. He didn't even really exist to me at all.

I've dreamed about this day, a chance to just pick up a father-daughter relationship where we are now and never have to remember the absent past, but sometimes it feels like we're made more for our pasts than for our dreams.

"What will you be having?" the waitress asks us after setting down a couple of glasses of water.

"Una cerveza, para mi. Tres tacos al pastor, y para ti, mija?" Dad says, reaching for a handful of chips to dip into the chunked salsa. Beer and three tacos full of pork definitely break Tío's rules, but Dad gives off the aura that he knows what he's doing, so I hope.

"Pork on the Full Moon?" I ask, to remind him if he forgot, but he simply grins through a mouthful of chips and salsa.

"Absolutely," Dad answers, through the chip crumbs over his upper lip stache.

"Umm... I guess I'll have two tacos de papas," I say, more unsure of myself than I thought I'd be. My stomach is cavernous, but Tío said moderation is important on the day of a Full Moon.

"Mija, no! Order something con carne! With meat! You'll need your strength for the upcoming night! Give her what I ordered!" he says without another thought.

"Thanks," I say to the waitress, and she smiles and disappears.

The more I look at him, the more I realize Dad actually looks like me. Our hair, his now thinner, has the same unruly curl. Our noses are the same Spanish points, compared to my mother's more indigenous straight nose. Our mannerisms and hand gestures are similar. Even the sweat beading across the top of his scalp from the spicy food is something my scalp always does. And, admittedly, I feel like my mom, sitting with me, as he talks a mile a minute to the point it's hard to focus, the way I do on my rambles. And the more I watch him, the less of Mom I feel inside myself. And, about that, I'm not sure how to feel.

"So, mija, tell me more about you! When do you graduate? Any interests, hobbies? Excited for your first hunt?" he says, pulling me out of my fog.

"Umm, well, I like to sketch and draw, and I love listening to music."

"Do you still dance, mija? You used to love to sing and dance when you were little."

I sink in my chair, blushing in disbelief that he still remembers that phase of my life. It seems easy for adults to just forget things from so long ago.

"No, I prefer the quiet escape of reading, to the nervous energy of performing in front of an audience," I say, my palms starting to sweat.

To that, Dad, *grunts?*

"No es bueno, that's not good mija. People need to hear your voice, and you used to love to dance. It made you so happy. Mija, I'm going to tell you something, and I'm only going to say this once: I know I've made a lot of mistakes in my life, as a husband and as a father, but one thing that I want you to learn from me is how to have fun. Everyone needs to learn how to let loose, especially those with our abilities. Come on, get up, we're dancing," he says, seeing me grow more confused the more he spoke.

Then he stands up and pulls me out of my seat toward the dance floor. The bachata starts, and dad sways his hips and moves along to the rhythm. I follow his lead, the way I did with mom in the bachata class we took together for mother-daughter bonding.

"Let's go, Selena! You won't let your namesake down, or let an old man dance all by himself, will you?"

I'm sure the waitresses and other guests are watching, but I go with it, being led by the corners of my smile. My fear, no match for Dad's confidence... that makes me feel... safe.

"If you tell anyone about this, I'm never doing it again," I say, laughing at my missteps as we dance.

"Deal!" he says. "We'll have to make next time with everyone else. As a family!"

"We'll have to see about that," I say. "I don't think Mom's danced since we had a picnic at the beach... When I was ten!"

"Ay, that hurts my heart, mija," he says, holding his chest.

Then he grabs my hands, and we sway to the sound of the music, moving to the Bachata without stepping on each other's feet. He's good at it, and I smile at the empty spot inside myself where our father-daughter quinceañera dance used to be, feeling it fill with the music around us and the feeling of his hands in mine. I almost don't want it to end.

But eventually, the song concludes, and the guests applaud. For me and Dad or for the music, I'm not sure. Then we head back to the table.

"Eso! That's it mija, you've still got it," Dad declares, proudly patting my arm across the table.

The smile is unstoppable on me.

"You know what, in the course of a day, the moon sets before the sun and rises to finish the night. Us Valencias are always in tune with that energy more than other families, and to also be a Sol... You are going to be unstoppable, mija. You just might eclipse me some day. I'll be right back. I have to use the bathroom, but think about that, mija. Think about your power."

As I sit back, thinking about my power, I take a few bites of the tacos that came while we were dancing. It's the first time I've eaten meat in, I can't remember how long, but it's tender and salty, and somehow more satisfying than I remember. But I'm not sure if it's the wolf or the girl in me that enjoys it more.

After a few bites, two men who look like they're in their forties start loitering around the table, and, seeing me alone, approach me.

"So, when's our turn, señorita?" the taller one with black cowboy boots and a matching cowboy hat says.

And my stomach drops like in an elevator ride.

"Oh, I'm not really a dancer," I say, searching the back of the restaurant for Dad.

"Look, let's not be strangers. Have a drink, on us!" says the shorter guy with dirty timberlands and a fluorescent orange vest.

"I don't drink. I'm only fi-fi-fi-fifteen," now full on panicking, to their apparent delight.

"She's just my type," the taller one says, slapping the other's arm. "She's cute when she gets flustered."

"I'm not interested in two gross old men like you," I snap, impressing myself with my strength.

"Aw, she's a little witchy one, ain't she?" the shorter says.

Then the taller steps closer and grabs my left wrist.

"It's okay, I like them feisty, too," he says with a smirk.

Now, I'm fuming hot and sweating bullets, and actually *wanting* the wolf inside me to come out. These guys don't know who they're messing with. *I'm* not even sure who they're dealing with. But I know, if they keep at it, eventually, I'm going to blow.

"I said I'm not interested. No, means no!"

And with a super-strong twist of my left wrist I gain control of the tall one, and push his elbow straight up until he cries out in pain. The exact way Tío Julio taught me after I told him meditation wasn't enough to prepare me for the world.

The taller one's off me, and I let him go, hoping he learned his lesson. Then the shorter guy tries to pick me up from behind, and I slack to make myself deadweight. It's not enough. He's stronger than he looks, but through my wolf hearing, I hear the bathroom door swing open. I know it's my father.

"Este güey, you better get your hands off my daughter!" he says.

Dad charges towards us from across the room like a bull, and I step on the construction worker's foot, then kick him in his crotch while he's distracted. The place Mom always told me to aim for if any old creep gets handsy.

"If you give her to us, we won't give you any trouble," the taller cowboy says, crossing his arms.

"Like hell I will," Dad says, walking up and connecting the guy with an uppercut to the jaw that sends him flat to the ground.

"Dad, let's get out of here," I say, pulling him away from prolonging the fight. But sirens are already in the distance and getting closer. Within minutes, all four of us are handcuffed against the wall outside.

"They started it," I say indignantly.

"Don't say a word until we get a phone call to a lawyer," says the cowboy to his friend.

Dad nods to what he says, so I lean back against the wall of the building and wait for what comes next. Even though it's a Mexican restaurant, with

Mexican staff, when the two guys claimed dad was responsible for starting the fight, the officers were inclined to believe them, over all of us.

I can't look at Dad as we're brought to separate cars for transport. If I were able to stop them myself, we might not be mixed up in all of this. I know he's the hero of the night, but watching them shut the bar-windowed car door, a fear plumes in my gut that the world might make him out to be the villain. And when they shut the door on me, I sit with that fear as the evening approaches sunset.

An hour and a half later, they book my father while I wait in another room.

"Please, let us go!" I plead to the officer filling out paperwork for the juvenile detention center.

"You don't know what will happen if we're not let out by sundown," I whisper.

"What, will you turn into a pumpkin? Should've thought of that before you and your father were drunk and disorderly picking a fight at the taco shop," says the surly Officer Eaton with his combed mullet and sunglasses clipped on his chest above his beer belly.

"Sorry, kid, you need to learn to find a better way to channel that aggression. Try Tai Chi, it's what my mother does, and it looks relaxing," says Officer Beckman, a female cop with a short pixie cut. Her stern face looks out of place with her baby-round eyes. Officer Eaton snatches the paperwork from my hands and scans it with a mixture of repugnance and superiority.

"The other officers should be here before you know it," Officer Beckman says, winking at me before turning away.

"What time?" I ask, feeling weak after not even getting the chance to finish eating my meal. Those guys ruined everything, but I find a little satisfaction in knowing they're getting booked, too. For what, though? I don't know.

"Maybe 6:00 or 7:00 pm," she says, and I get worried.

By then, it will be too late to get safely back to Tío's. After a few agonizing minutes of struggling against the rising wolf inside of me, I hear squeaky booted footsteps in the hallway, and the door creaks open.

"Ms. Valencia, my name is Officer Ford. I'm here to collect you. Would you stand up, please?" he says in a firm but professional manner.

"Yes, please," I sigh in relief. "Get me out of here."

"We're not quite at that stage yet, but I'll get you moving in the right direction. I just sat with your dad. He's aware of everything that's going on."

"Where is he?" I ask. "I want to see him. It's not right to separate parents and children."

"He's on his way to where we're transporting you to. It's all in the agreement laid out with him."

"What about the kidnappers?" I ask, needing answers. If I were the police, those guys would be my prime suspects for the missing girls cases.

"They're in their own processes," Ford says, looking over at the other officer. "She's a talkative one, huh?"

"All the kids are these days," Officer Beckman says.

"You coming?" Ford asks.

"Fine," I say, looking between the two officers suspiciously, and follow him out the door. There's not much of a choice anymore.

My handcuffs clink like a commercial jingle as I follow Ford down the sterile, stone precinct halls. It's echo, forever the tune of my walk towards freedom, or to my potential demise. It's a strange feeling to worry about those around you, and yourself, not surviving the night.

Outside, he takes me to the curb where his black, unmarked, SUV is parked, and I climb in. The leather is smooth against my legs and arms where my skin touches, and I'm thankful I haven't gone full hairy and ripped Ford's head off... yet. I need to know where Dad's being taken before I can even think about... turning. But the sun is setting, and the moon is rising. And I feel the danger of myself simmering.

"Listen, sir, I know you're just doing what you're supposed to, but you need to release me or something terrible is going to happen tonight!" I try pleading.

"You gonna turn into the moon or something?" he asks.

"Something like that! I'm a woman now!"

"Listen, missy, I've heard it all before. Don't worry, we're going somewhere you'll fit in... with all the other girls who are 'women' too."

"What do you mean?" I ask.

And he hits the accelerator harder. The SUV speeds over road lines and nearly drifts around bends as the night grows dimmer. I'm jerked from side to side, with no way to buckle myself in. I try to open the door, to jump out, but it's a useless effort.

"You're not really a cop, driving like *this* are you?" I ask, growing more worried the further away from civilization we drive.

"Both can be true, but the real question is, where are we going?" he says, smirking at me in the rearview mirror.

"To where all the other kidnapped girls went?!" I shriek.

"Well, why ruin the surprise?" he settles on, the air around us growing icy.

"You'll be the one in for a surprise, tonight!" I say, kicking at the back of his seat as the rage boils inside me.

"Stop it!" he says. "Or I'll have your father killed, and there'll be nothing you can do about it!"

I stop, but I don't take my eyes off his eyes in the rearview mirror. I want him to see the sheer fury that I want to unleash on him.

"You're gonna come easily," Ford says, parking the SUV in front of a large house down a dirt road. The sun is in its final seconds of setting, but the night sky looks like it's going to be bright above the darkness of the forest. I search for life inside the house, but find not a light on or shade raised. Then Ford's hand is around my mouth with some kind of damp cloth, and everything falls away to a shimmering blackness

When I finally come to, my head is a pounding pain, my tongue feels like a dry sea sponge, and I can barely see anything through the blur of my unfocused vision. But one sense is as sharp as ever, and I unmistakably smell a horse. Dry hay along the floors itches me through my clothes and pierces my bleeding, now tied-behind-my-back hands.

A rustling comes from somewhere, but I can't tell if it's somewhere around me or out of sight. My blurred vision is making it hard to place the sound, and I'm not sure if it's someone to help or someone to hurt me.

"Is anyone out there?!" I cry, feeling powerless as my body shakes off whatever Ford knocked me out with.

"Yeah, they got you too," I hear a young woman's voice, and see a figure come closer to my face.

"Who are you? What's your name?" I blink furiously, to hopefully see.

"Maria," she whispers.

"Where are we?" I ask.

"We don't know," she says.

"Who's we?"

"Me and the other girls."

"The missing girls? How old are you, Maria?"

"I'm sixteen, how old are you?"

"I just turned fifteen," I say.

"You better get out of here if you know what's best for you," she whispers. "These people are not normal farmers... They're human traffickers. I'm the girl that went missing a week ago. Their plan is to collect teenage girls and sell us off to the highest bidder on the black market. Their dairy semi-truck isn't filled with milk, it's filled with girls."

"Eww, gross," I cry, forgetting to whisper as my skin crawls. "Do you have a knife or something? I need to get my hands free."

"No," Maria says.

"Hmmm, well... I might have something that will work. I'm going to need you to slap me."

"Seriously?" she asks.

"Yes, please smack me! I can't be here anymore!"

"Sure..." she says, taking a step back. "If it'll help. Ready?"

"Okay..." I say, and I wait for it. She smacks my cheek... hard. Bringing tears to my eyes and bruising my jaw, but that's it. No transformation.

"Again! Harder!" I say, feeling something stirring in me.

Maria slaps again, and this time the metallic taste of blood floods my mouth.

I hit the ground, and all of my senses start coming back to me. Maria *is* a teenage girl, and her pretty brown hair is matted like a barn child's. Bruises mark her arms, but the fear in her eyes looks completely because of me, as my claws dig into the barn wood floor.

"You need to get out of here quick and get some help," I say, cutting her wrist-binds with one of my were-nails.

"What about you?" she asks, looking at my claws. "Are you okay?"

"I need to get as far away from people as possible!" I say, anxious about getting out under the moon.

"Got it!" Maria says, running out of our barn stall and to the four girls across from us. They all leave through a side door in the back, and I go to leave out the door on the other side to make sure I stay far away from them. I struggle through the pain of my body, and make it out of the stall. But before I reach the back door, I hear the familiar voice of a woman coming down the other end of the stables. So, I hide around a couple of horses who, thankfully, aren't spooked by my claws.

"Where did those girls go?" the woman says. Could it be, Sheri? No, not possible.

"I don't know, I left them right here!" says a familiar male voice, maybe... John? No way!

"You idiot, did you not tie them tight enough? God, I swear I have to do everything myself," the venomous woman says.

"I'm sorry... What do you want me to do about it? Go back in time?" he asks.

"Look for them!" she barks. "They couldn't've gotten far. You, search outside."

And I hear her heels clicking into every stable.

Shit, I think.

She's getting closer, and about to find me, so I move through the shadows to the other side of the barn, staying out of sight.

"Oh, little girls, where are you?" she says in her sing-song southern accent. There's no doubt it's Sheri. I cover my face with my hair and try to blend in, holding my breath. I hear her move around, closer, closer, and... then move away.

"Really, Selena, you shouldn't have gotten up at all," comes the voice of Sheri Lynn Butler a few feet in front of me, and I jump for the bucket at my feet.

"Don't come any closer! I'm dangerous!" I say, watching her in the glow of the moonlight from outside.

"Oh, I don't think you know what real danger is," she smiles, showing teeth, stomping her boot against the wooden floor.

"You don't understand," I say, avoiding her steps, moving us in a circular motion. "If I'm not home before the Full Moon is exact, something terrible is going to happen!"

"Don't threaten me, little girl," she says, her voice getting sharper.

That's when she turns, and I spot a gun in a holster.

"You wouldn't have silver bullets in that gun, would you?" I ask.

"No, why?" she asks, lines appearing on her forehead.

"'Cause, now it's a fair-fight," I say, channeling all my energy into an elbow strike to Sheri's side, just as Tío taught me, and send her sprawling back.

"She's in here!" Sheri struggles to shout out. "She's getting away!" she gasps, and I think about my next steps.

Someone outside closes the doors to the barn, effectively trapping me inside with her... and her gun. Which she grabs for and points at me. And for once, I don't feel fear, but rage. I thrash my claws, and get her arms pinned to the ground. Everything in me wants to rip her to pieces. A child trafficker?! How could she?

"Scratch me, slash my throat! I know you want to! You're just an animal after all! Who else could you be? You're that *freak's* niece!" she spits.

"Me! An animal? You lock girls up, transport them to God knows where for torture! And *I'm* the animal?" I growl.

"I provide for my family!" Sheri shouts. "The government stopped giving us subsidies for our dairy farm. Do you know how expensive cows are these days? How else could I pay for the farm?!" she says. "Plus, it's become a lucrative community business, as you can tell."

In the heat of rage, the transformation rips through my body, and pain bursts out with every new bulging muscle and hair follicle that pierces my bloody skin. My bones break out of place, and dislocate into new places. Fur sprouts *everywhere*, and Sheri looks at me with more disgust in her eyes than I'd ever seen before. But I smile my sharp toothed wolf-girl smile through the pain, and what was fear, turns to strength. Sheri scrambles across the floor for her gun, and I take off on all fours, leaping between shots as I flee across the barn and out into the woods.

Running as a were-girl is like moving while the rest of the world is in slow motion. The Blue Moon sits above the forest, lighting up the night through the tree branches. When I finally get to a mossy hill, I find the moon in full, and I take in its power-giving rays with a long, blissful howl. Some kind of instinct pulls from me all the sorrow deep down inside, and

I let it out into the night. Tears stream, and I howl as my body—were-body, stretches itself out with every cry.

Then, I hear a howl back, and somehow it's familiar.

12

CLAW FIGHTS AND FUR

After some time of running, my mind goes blank, and I'm left with tranquility. I hear the howl again. But for some reason, I know no one is coming to save me. I'm the one who needs to do the saving. I run, and if someone sees me from a distance, they would never believe I'm a girl who needs an inhaler to climb up a flight of stairs sometimes. I leap over fences and dodge the farm dogs in pursuit... of what? I'm not sure. Until, I find a dairy truck sitting in an open field. *The rest of the girls. I can still save them.*

I run up next to the tanker, scouting the field as I go. Nobody's around, so I lurch my way up and pop open the manhole. Inside, I find at least five more girls, who all scream when they see me. I howl, and one stands in front of the rest, looking up at me in the spotlight of moonlight.

"She won't hurt us. I trust her more than I trust that vieja," she says, and they all start climbing. "In my mother's pueblo, in Mexico, they had legends of la Loba," she says, steady as she climbs. "I never thought they were true. I never thought I'd meet one touched by la Loba. Thank you, friend! Go! We'll be fine from here!"

Atop the next hill, I look back to see the girls all running for the freeway, where someone will see them and help them. Like I did. I saved them all. Even with the lobo inside, making me wonder more about why some werewolves were hunters and why some aren't. I might not have control of my wereform, but it's certainly not turning me into a murderer.

My inner lobo, somehow, sniffs my way back home, and I make it to Tío's with the Blue Moon still high over the farm. And somewhere inside, I hear Mom's voice!?

"You can't do this! Why are you doing this!?" she asks in a panic.

"Your daughter's seen too much, and as selfish as she is, I know she wouldn't want anything to happen to you or your monstrous brother. I could sell him on the black market, too, come to think of it. I wonder how much a werewolf would sell for," Sheri says. "I've only heard rumored figures."

"She's not coming back, she's smarter than that," Mom says, just as I burst through the door.

"Ay, mija! I spoke too soon," Mom says, slumping her shoulders in her binds, to the amusement of Sheri.

"Finally, the girl we've been waiting for. You going to play nice, or am I going to make this a family affair?" she says, grinning.

I growl back, my lips curling over my fangs.

"Boys, get her already! What are you doing?" she says.

That's when I see him, John. Holding a tranquilizer gun standing beside the two traffickers from the restaurant! All lunging at me.

Through my wolf eyes, John's skin isn't flawless. It's thin and frail. I could easily slash his throat with my claws, throw him across the room, or rip into his skin with my teeth. The blood pulsing through their veins as they struggle to pin me down is almost telling me to do it. Convincing me to get a taste.

"This isn't a girl anymore!" the tall one says, wrestling against the strength of one of my arms as he tries to wrestle my unmoving form.

"She's a monster!" the short one says, going for my knees, but neither of them is enough to take me down now.

"You mean...? Selena...? That's you?" John says, finally connecting the dots as wetness sprouts like roots down his legs.

Then he pulls the trigger of the tranq dart, pointed at me, and I yank the short guy into the way.

"Agh," he cries, before his weight goes slack from the dart in his back. I throw him back at John, sending both of them in a heap to the floor. Then, I shove the tall one off into the wall behind me.

"You losers!" Sheri cries, shaking before leaping across the room for the tranquilizer gun.

"Mija!" Mom yells, as the dart whizzes past my neck.

"You should've stayed gone," she hisses, cocking the gun again.

"You should stop, Sheri—," Mom pleads, her makeup streaking down her cheeks.

Then the front door creaks open, and a shadow looms in. In a flash of fur there's a snarl, a pounce, and Sheri's screams. It's Tío—no longer human. I use my claws to rip Mom free from her binds, and we move away as Sheri's screams dissolve into silence. Were-Tío, our savior. Bloody, brave, and breathing heavy through his sharp toothed snout. And the unrecognizable beast inside of him howls.

Tall guy and John run out into the fields, leaving only the lifeless Sheri and unconscious short guy left. Then Tío leaps through the kitchen window and out into the night.

"Mija... you're changed," Mom says, looking me over.

I offer a heartfelt howl, and Mom starts to pray. Under her breath comes Psalm 23, in Spanish. Her hands tremble in a frantic rhythm as she prays, while I stare up into her eyes through ones I'm surprised she recognizes.

"The Lord is my shepherd; I shall not want. He maketh me to lie down in green pastures: he leadeth me beside the still waters."

My breathing steadies.

"He restores my soul: he leads me in the paths of righteousness for his name's sake."

My eyes grow heavy.

"Yea, though I walk through the valley of the shadow of death, I will fear no evil: for thou art with me; your rod and your staff, they comfort me.

"You prepare a table before me in the presence of mine enemies: you anoint my head with oil; my cup runs over."

I feel myself somewhere between conscious and unconscious.

"Surely goodness and mercy shall follow me all the days of my life: and I will dwell in the house of the Lord forever."

And I nod off, my throat thick with heat. My jaw, tight. Nails, no, claws digging into my palms.

EPILOGUE

MOONLIGHT & MEDICATION

The courtroom is cold, in the way all sterile places are. No windows, no breeze. Just still air and quiet judgment. My wrists itch, the restraints an unpleasant reminder that I'm in the criminal justice system. The judge shuffles through a stack of papers. He makes slow, deliberate sounds, like he's trying to fill the silence with authority. I focus on them to stay steady.

"And the final recommendation," the judge says, eyes scanning the print, "is that the defendant receive immediate outpatient psychiatric care with a new medication protocol and community service, to be completed upon clinical clearance."

A pause.

"Three weeks minimum at a therapeutic facility, followed by re-evaluation."

No mention of claws. No mention of howling. No talk of the blood. Just mania and hallucinations. Just labels. A rabid wolf took out Sheri, that's what witnesses say. All of us.

"Bipolar I Disorder, with psychotic features."

Across the courtroom, John's fidgeting at the end of the bench and avoiding my gaze. His testimony reduced to stammering nonsense and urine-stained pants when he got to the rabid wolf part. But he made everyone laugh, after he said I growled at him.

As for the girls? Brave as ever.

They deny seeing anything that night except me, a human girl, freeing them from captivity. Thankfully, heroics kept Tío from prosecution, but because of the reports of me 'attacking' customers at the bar and causing a disturbance, even though everyone involved was corrupt, I still had to face some form of legal proceeding.

Every one of them pointed to her name when the photos were laid out, corroborating my story.

Sheri Lynn Butler: Head of the Vacaville child trafficking ring.

Gone.

Only blood stains and bloody bones were found.

The rest of her disappeared like fog in the morning sun.

The judge thanks the girls, and thanks my mother for her 'honesty,' thanks my public defender for her 'compassionate framing of mental health in underrepresented communities.'

He even thanked Dad earlier, before he was let off for self defense, after spending the night as a werewolf in a cell (alone thankfully). But he was sent to be transported back to Mexico for release.

No one thanks me, but the girls mouth it to me from their stand. And by the look on Daisy's face, she's nothing but proud of me.

The facility isn't far from the farm. A few hours away, the beach house/rehab is located between mountains and the ocean. My mom squeezes my hand before the guards escort me out of the courtroom.

"Three weeks," she says, voice thick. "We'll come every Sunday. Tu tío también."

He stands behind her, clean-shaven, collared shirt, eyes down.

"Don't worry, I'll feed Luna while you're gone. Your mom will be in your old room, and we'll work on building another room for you," he says, and winks. "Just remember what I taught you. You'll get out right before the next... "

Then guards walk me out.

The door closes behind me.

And even as the lights hum and the carpet exudes the smell of bleach, somewhere in the distance, I swear I hear it.

A low howl, not of pain, but of remembrance and the light of a new beginning.

THE END

LIVIN' LA VIDA LLORONA

Selena Sol-Valencia
Episodio 2

by

Angelica Martinez

COMING AUGUST 2026

SUBSCRIBE TO NEWSLETTER FOR COVER REVEAL

FourElementsPress.com

Learn about the Press Mission of uplifting marginalized voices, and support us as we grow to support more creatives in manifesting their dreams into your hands.

AUTHOR'S NOTE

This is a love letter to my Mexican-American experience, and how I wouldn't live it any other way. The drama, the gossip, café, y comida. The way we love one another and stick together through our best and our worst. I love it all, and I hope these hundred pages make you fall in love, too.

Selena's story started with the telling of my own. I have struggled with mood disorders since turning fifteen. In the same year, my grandmother passed away, alongside my childhood pet cat. It was also the year my dad left us and moved back to Mexico. The shock to my nervous system was unbearable, and as I struggled to process the grief, suicidal ideations became my daily battle.

Eventually, I was diagnosed with anxiety and major depressive disorder. As I grew into adulthood, I would go on to collect the diagnoses of ADHD, PTSD, Bipolar 1, and Autism (Level 1). While I never received a diagnosis of being a werewolf, I have always empathized with the plight of werewolves unable to control themselves due to external factors: the Full Moon, bodily mutations, etc.. As humans, we rarely have control of our environment, but we do have control of ourselves. Even in the midst of mania, I made choices to save my life and the lives of others by vocalizing my pain.

Often in Latino culture, mental illness is met with horror, judgment, and secret keeping. I hope this book helps spark conversation around removing stigma from mental health. We have to remove the stigma away from needing and asking for help. We are raised to be self-sufficient, always serving others, and smiling through pain without a hair out of place. Quinceañeras, in particular, hold great cultural significance, making them the perfect setting to let loose and unleash the madness within.

This book was very cathartic for me to write. In life, I didn't have the same courage to 'break all the rules' like Selena, but you could say I went through my rebellious phase later in life. This book is for the courageous teens and wallflowers inside of all of us. Let no one silence your voice. It is your most potent weapon.

I mean it when I say, the pen is mightier than the sword.

Thank you, and until next time,

Angelica Martinez

LIVIN' LA VIDA LOBA

BOOK CLUB READERS' GUIDE

This Episodio of La Vida Selena Sol-Valencia is a story read best with loved ones! Here are a few questions to help guide you through book club conversations!

• In what ways does the text show cultural influence in the decisions characters make, and how do the characters reflect on those moments? Think, Selena, Julio, Mom, Dad?

• In what ways does Selena cope with change, and are all of those ways positive?

• Neurodivergent life is portrayed in the media in mixed ways, but in reality it is often experienced as personality features, both subjectively and objectively, making behavioral patterns difficult to identify. In many ways, help comes for Selena, but is that help good enough?

- This text tackles the very real horrors of corruption, child trafficking, and the generational impacts of colonization. In what ways does their presence impact the daily lives of our characters?

- What moral questions come up around killings done by werewolves, opposed to the intentional criminal activity of the child traffickers?

- This text tracks the inheritance of mental disorders like anxiety and bipolar alongside a werewolf curse and how those challenges are treated specifically within Latino culture. What are some challenges in yourself or your family/culture that are similar and different? How do those challenges manifest in your daily/yearly life?

- Youth who suffer are often disciplined instead of treated, emphasizing the role of mental health education and services for both parents and children through outlets like schools. Do you see more of a need for such services in your communities?

LIVIN' LA VIDA LOBA

FOR THE WEREWOLF TRACKERS

- Are you more of a North of the border, solo type lone-wolf? Or more of a community-oriented South of the border werewolf?

- Would you prefer turning all at one, or for the change to gradually overtake you, as you approach your first transformation?

- Would you follow Julio's rules, or let your wolf spirit fly free?

- During transformation, is the person or the lobo in control? What does that say about Selena? What does that say about Tío Julio?

- Do you believe Selena will get to a place of control enough to follow all of Tío Julio's rules to tame her inner lobo?

- Is the judge in on the conspiracy? And is Selena safe?

Notes

Notes

LIVIN' LA VIDA LLORONA

Selena Sol-Valencia
Episodio 2

AUGUST 2026

by

Angelica Martinez

Join the Email List for Updates:

FourElementsPress.com

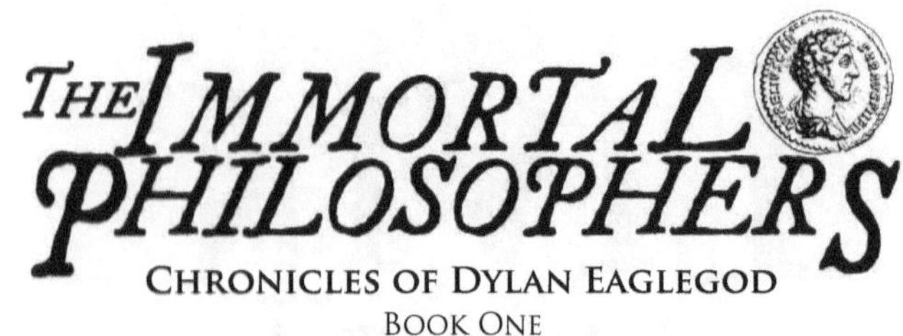

CHRONICLES OF DYLAN EAGLEGOD
BOOK ONE

SUNSET IN THE VALLEY OF NOW AND THEN

OUT NOW

CHRONICLES OF DYLAN EAGLEGOD
BOOK TWO

LOST BETWEEN THE LANDS OF HERE AND THERE

Spring 2026

Discover the world of The Immortal Philosophers as Dylan Eaglegod battles for survival against the monsters of his old life.

by

ALEXANDER ANTHONY CASILLAS

Join the Email List for Updates:

FourElementsPress.com

TheImmortalPhilosophers.com

FOUR
ELEMENTS
PRESS

www.ingramcontent.com/pod-product-compliance
Lightning Source LLC
Chambersburg PA
CBHW031543310726
48971CB00008B/2597